Your Life, My Life

June Emerson

BOOKS BY THE SAME AUTHOR

Reflections in the Nile
(extracts appear in 'Unsuitable for Ladies' by Jane Robinson)

Albania – The Search for the Eagle's Song

Ladies, Gentlemen or Whatever

The Music of Albania

All proceeds from sales go to Ryedale Carers' Support
(www.ryedalecarers.org.uk)

Cover design Sandra Oakins
with detail from 'Indian Blue' by June Emerson

Contents

1. Noël bangs his head

Noël Burke cautiously felt the tender spot on his head. No blood. Good. He moved a couple of chairs out so that, in future, he couldn't walk under the cast-iron spiral staircase.

'Time to begin,' he said briskly to himself and pulled forward a clean pad of paper. It was good to be writing by hand again. He'd purposely left the laptop behind for the week so that he could enjoy complete isolation. A gaggle of cheerful Yorkshire voices came and went past the thick oak door, and the twice-daily train ground its way off into the hills. Then silence.

It had been a bit of luck finding this place at the last minute. He'd gone online and found The Stationmaster's Office at Holtby Monkton. Stone-flagged, one-up-one-down, connected by the spiral staircase on which he'd just dented his skull. The builders were starting work on Treetops this week. Mike was safely in a Quaker care home for a month. Noël needed time to sort out his thoughts.

He put his pen down and felt his head again. This sore spot on his head was rather like the major worry on his mind. Mike. Mike was a good friend. Mike had a genial sense of humour and was never unkind. Mike had suffered a stroke four years ago. Mike had come to live with Noël the previous year – and it was not as easy as he had anticipated.

Mike's memory and cognition had suffered after the stroke. It was enough to make his life sometimes confusing and alarming, sometimes full of innocent joy. Since his fall back in the summer he was much more wobbly on his legs and his short term memory had deteriorated. Things were getting tricky.

'I'll camp out in the kitchen while the builders are in,' Noël had said to Beth and Eddie.

'Why don't you take a complete break? You're looking very strained these days.'

'Oh I'm fine. It'll be interesting to see how they change that gloomy entrance hall into something light and pleasant.'

'Noël,' said Beth looking him in the eye, 'take a break. They'll only be tearing stuff out for the first week and it'll be hell to live with.'

'Pity you can't stay with us on the boat,' said Eddie. 'But with Margot bombing around, and Beth feeding the twins at night, you wouldn't have much peace.'

After he'd left Mike at the care home yesterday afternoon, and eventually settled down in the stationmaster's armchair with a cup of tea, he had felt all the sinews in his body gradually begin to loosen. He hadn't realised how tense he had been. He tried not to remember Mike's last remark as he'd left him at the Quaker care home:

'I expect you'll be glad to be shot of me for a while.'

'You're in absolutely the right place while all this bloody chaos is going on! I daresay you'll be spoilt rotten by the staff too.'

His cheery words sounded cheap, and he left quickly, feeling terrible.

2. A bit of history

It was when he'd been appointed full-time Arts Correspondent on *The Voice of the North* that they had first met. Mike had been principal oboe in the Hallé Orchestra in Manchester and Noël had often gone to the pub with the players after concerts. Some of the choice phrases about a visiting conductor, or a mind-bending new work, had been useful to Noël. Descriptive adjectives, particularly from the brass section, had to be considerably toned-down, but it helped to have a view from in front of, as well as behind, the podium. He and Mike had other interests in common too, most specifically boats, and gradually a strong friendship had built up. Noël had left London after his disastrous marriage to Beryl had come to an end. Sometimes after a late concert Noël would stay overnight with Mike and his wife Mary in Manchester rather than drive back to Ripon. Mike and Mary were comfortable to be with and their home had a relaxing effect on him.

Noël had always dreamed of living on a boat, but Beryl wouldn't hear of it. When they finally divorced he sold their rather prissy little flat in Highgate and became the proud owner of Archimedes – the butt of many a bawdy joke from the Hallé trombone section. She was 30 feet long – yes Archimedes had to be female – with a spacious saloon, a double and a single cabin and a narrow galley. She was moored on what remained of the Ripon Canal, not far from the Cathedral. It was sheer joy, after a concert, to step down into the saloon, light the little Calor gas stove and settle down to write up his notes. It was utterly peaceful. There were no mocking remarks and intrusive questions to deal with.

'I think I've always been a loner really,' he had said to Mike once. 'I enjoy my own company. That's probably what made Beryl so ratty. She wanted me to be involved with everything she did. If I took myself off for a while she was resentful. Worst of all she had no time for classical music.

'Well I find you good company,' said Mike. 'But then we blokes generally allow each other to be ourselves.'

'It's not just blokes,' said Noël. 'Mary doesn't expect you to get involved in her tapestry workshops.'

'True,' agreed Mike. 'She doesn't fuss about my oboe reeds either, so long as I don't leave scrapings all over the kitchen table.'

Noël's visits to Manchester had become less frequent as *The Voice of the North* began cutting back their arts coverage. They didn't want to lose Noël though, so they added book reviews and some more general features to his brief, which suited him well. This meant that he saw less of Mike and Mary and, after Mike retired from the orchestra, several years passed with no more than the occasional e-mail and Christmas card.

It was about three years ago that Noël went to cover an important World Première given by the Hallé. He liked the Bridgewater Hall, its angled glass frontage reared up like the prow of a ship. It was light and airy inside, served good coffee and overlooked the Bridgewater Canal. As he sat with his coffee before the concert someone clapped him on the shoulder.

'Hi Noël!' boomed a familiar voice, and Stefan Kovacs dumped his bassoon case and sat plumply down.

'Hi Stefan!' said Noël, wiping his knee where the coffee had spilt. 'So long since I've seen you. How's the band these days?'

'Going well,' said Stefan. 'We've had some tricky times, as you know, and some really weird conductors.' Here he paused to roll his eyes and give a big Hungarian guffaw. 'Why don't you come so much now we're in this great new hall?'

'The Cuts,' said Noël, rolling his eyes too, but not as gloriously as Stefan. 'The paper can't afford to send me out so often.'

'Too bad,' said Stefan. 'You miss a lot of good jokes. Did you know that a violin and a viola are actually the same size?'

'OK. Go on. Tell me…'

'It's just that the viola players have smaller heads!' Stefan nearly rolled off his chair.

'How's the new first oboe?' asked Noël after he'd wiped his eyes. 'Not so new now I suppose. Mike's been retired quite a while.'

'She's great,' said Stefan. 'Studied with Holliger you know. Gorgeous sound. Mike's not so good though.'

Noël straightened up, alert. 'Why? What's happened?'

Stefan was suddenly serious. 'Mary was taken ill with cancer. Mike insisted on looking after her to the end. Then he got a stroke.'

'Is he dead?' gasped Noël, horrified that he hadn't known anything of this.

'No, he's OK,' said Stefan, 'but he couldn't manage on his own so he's living in an old-people's home.'

'Oh God! Not that,' groaned Noël.

There had been a lot of unpleasant news about care homes in the papers recently. In today's world it seems that old people have become a commodity, to be dealt with. They've become a problem, a 'growing problem'. The State cares for the poorer ones as cheaply as it can. The well-heeled see their life-savings flow swiftly into the pockets of businessmen. Children visit their parents guiltily and hastily while struggling to keep their feet on the work and property ladder.

'Oh God!' said Noël again as all this flashed like headlines through his mind.

Stefan leaned across and put an arm round his shoulders. 'Hey Noël. It's OK,' he said gently. 'Some of the guys have been going over to see him. The stroke wasn't too bad. He can talk fine, he can walk with a stick. His memory's a bit scrappy.'

'Why couldn't Edgar take him in?' asked Noël incredulously. Mike's son Edgar worked for an oil company and was pretty well off.

'Edgar's in Nigeria now,' said Stefan. 'No place for his old dad. He came over to sort things out, but he's got a contract he can't afford to break.'

'How long's Mike been in there?'

'It all happened about six months ago,' said Stefan. 'Tell you what. After the concert we'll meet up at the usual place for a drink and I'll give you all the details – phone number, address. OK?'

'Thanks,' said Noël and flopped back in his chair. 'Thanks Steffi.'

3. Visiting Mike

When Noël first went to visit Mike in the Peacehaven Care Home he was shocked to see how diminished his old friend seemed. He was sitting in an armchair in the lounge, by the window, staring into space.

'At least he isn't parked in front of the telly,' thought Noël, whose antipathy to the 'idiot box' was legendary. He went over, sat down in the chair opposite Mike and leaned forward.

'Hi there Mike,' he said gently, and waited.

Mike's eyes took some time to focus, then they widened gradually.

'It's you!' he croaked, and his face lit up. 'It's Old Nole!' Mike had never managed to give Noël his full two syllables.

'I've come to take you out to tea,' said Noël. He couldn't wait to get away from the overheated lethargy of the place. They walked slowly, arm in arm, to the front door where Matron waited with Mike's coat.

'Supper is at 5.30,' she said, 'so please get him back in good time.'

'That won't give us long. Isn't 5.30 a bit early to be called supper?'

'It's so the kitchen staff can get home early,' said Matron.

Noël suppressed his annoyance. Whose benefit is this place being run for, he thought, ungrammatically.

Over tea and toasted tea-cakes they picked up some of the threads of their lives. Mike told him about Mary's last months, now and again drifting off to other topics, or humming to himself. Noël told him how Archimedes had begun to show her age.

'She needs so much doing to her now – I'm going to have to sell her to someone who can do the work. I'm no handyman.

'That's sad,' said Mike. You were always happy on the water.

'True,' said Noël, 'but common sense, plus *anno domini* – I'm planning to move back into Treetops.

'Isn't that where your parents live?' asked Mike.

'They did, but Dad died last year and Mum's gone to live with my sister Stella in Sussex. Houses aren't selling just now, so it makes sense to live there even though it's so huge.'

6

Mike had stopped listening and his eyelids were drooping.

'Let's get back,' said Noël, 'or Matron will spank us!'

Mike came to with a giggle. Yes, there was plenty of the old Mike left.

4. Moving on

The next couple of years were a time of transition for Noël. 'Moving on to the next stage of life' he said to himself ruefully. A buyer was eventually found for Archimedes. Beth and Eddie were young and energetic. They wanted to live apart from the rat race, to live simply and do their own thing. Eddie was a skilled craftsman and could earn good money, but he chose to work for three days only each week. The rest of the time he spent with Beth or on his allotment.

'And now I'll be working on Archimedes,' he said with great satisfaction. 'We grow most of our own grub,' said Eddie. 'Beth's a fantastic cook. Most of our friends don't realise they're eating veggie when they come round.' Beth and Eddie's dream was to get Archimedes into tip-top condition and then start a family.

'I want my kids to grow up away from the telly and video games,' said Beth. 'I want them to breathe fresh air, to think for themselves and be self-reliant.'

'What about the other kids they'll meet at school?' asked Noël. 'Won't they think they're odd?'

'They won't be odd,' laughed Beth, 'just open and friendly. Able to talk about stuff. I've worked in schools for years helping the backward ones with their reading. Once they can read, I tell them, they can do anything. I just don't understand adults who say I can't cook, or I can't sew. If you can read you can cook, or sew, or learn Arabic!'

'It's a matter of wanting to, I suppose,' said Noël.

'That's it. People are encouraged to pay other people to do things for them. It turns the wheels of commerce.'

'She's off!' said Eddie, but Noël could see the admiration in his eyes. He was happy that Archimedes would have an interesting new life with this eager couple.

The first night at Treetops was dismal. All his belongings from the boat were heaped up in the gloomy entrance hall. It was one of those massive villas build by a Victorian industrialist to impress his rivals. Noël's great-grandfather had been in the lead-mining business. Most of his wealth seemed to have been put into the ground floor. The bedrooms were very plain in comparison. Maybe funds had run low by the time they got to the top floor. As a final act of defiance however a roaring lion, in terra cotta, thrust its face forward pugnaciously from the top gable. It seemed to warn those who came up the drive that the master of this house meant business.

Noël's father had always apologised for the lion when new visitors came. 'He means no harm,' he would say mildly. 'Making that ugly face just helps him to feel brave.'

'I know some people like that!' remarked more than one of his colleagues from the University.

Opening off the hall were three large rooms and a passage through to the kitchen. The bay window in the lounge looked out over the eponymous treetops to the misty city below. On the opposite side of the hall was the panelled library – a feather in the cap of any businessman, but a blessing to Noël and his father. Two-thirds of the books were his father's science library and University material, but a generous third was Noël's. Here he kept his music books and scores, dictionaries in several languages and centrally, like a row of pillars was a complete set of The New Grove Dictionary of Music – the musicians' bible. No room for all that on a narrow-boat! Although Noël could find most of the facts online that he needed for his work he still cherished time spent with the well-edited printed word.

'I expect you've got a huge CD collection too,' said Eddie, who had been helping with the move and was being shown round.

'Not really,' said Noël. 'A couple of dozen maybe.'

'I thought you were in the classical music business.'

'Yes, but it's live music I like,' replied Noël. 'The excitement of eighty talented players putting together, on the spot, the tapestry of sound created by a composer. There's a thrill and almost a danger – and every performance is different. CDs are manufactured and predictable.'

'That surprises me,' said Eddie, scratching his head. 'Don't you ever feel, like, I could just do with a bit of Mozart or something?'

'It may be old-fashioned of me, but I feel that music is too special to have it 'on tap' like beer. I like a bit of serendipity.'

'Never heard of him,' said Eddie.

'Sometimes I turn on the radio,' continued Noël, not wanting to embarrass Eddie, 'and there's a piece playing that I absolutely love. It fits my mood, there's time to savour it. It's a gift.'

'Well if you had it on CD you could have that gift whenever you fancied it,' said Eddie, forever practical.

'A gift is something you're given. It's usually a wonderful surprise. A gift isn't something you grab for yourself whenever you feel peckish!' Noël could see that he was beginning to sound pompous, so he turned and grinned at Eddie.

'I will admit something to you though.'

'What's that?'

Noël went to a drawer and took out a CD of Brahms String Quartets. 'That one, the one in C minor. I sometimes put that on, not often mind you, and then sit down and cry my eyes out.'

'Why's that?'

'I knew a cellist once…' said Noël. 'I'll say no more!' and he slapped Eddie on the shoulder. 'Thanks for all your help. I'll come down and see how you're getting on with Archimedes soon. Don't forget – he's a she.'

'Course not!' said Eddie. 'Bye now.'

The third room was a dining-room. Noël couldn't remember ever eating there as a child except on Christmas Day. There had always been a big Christmas tree in the bay window and he and Stella would decorate it together on her birthday, December 18th, which was exactly a week before Christmas Day.

'Keep Christmas short and special,' his father said. He got very cross with the shops that put up decorations earlier each year. The tree reflected its lights many times in the diamond panes and in the big mirror on the opposite wall over the fireplace.

'The tree goes on for ever and ever,' sighed Stella, her eyes wide. Yet Stella's birthday tea-party was always held in the kitchen, as was every other meal. Noël's birthday was on December 27th. This marked the end of the Burke family celebrations for the year. He'd been born a couple of days late to merit his name, but he got it anyway.

In contrast to the dark panelling of the three 'public' rooms and the entrance hall, the kitchen was light and bright. It spanned the whole width of the back of the house with windows looking out to the garden and between the pine trees to the fields beyond. At one end was a double-sized cooking range. Far too big for just the four of them, but it kept the room warm and suited its proportions. At the other end was a long farmhouse table, with a settle along one side and an assortment of wooden chairs. Two carvers, with broad arms and coloured padded cushions, were where the parents sat, one at each end. Mother sat at the business end, as she put it. The two children had occupied the settle, skidding along its polished seat. Sometimes they sat close together, conspiring, sometimes at opposite ends when they were annoyed with each other. The settle seat lifted up in three parts, and the space underneath was useful for cricket bats, fishing rods and other paraphernalia. Stella sometimes hid her sweets in the box with the tennis balls, and sometimes Noël pinched them.

'Now then, enough nostalgia,' said Noël out loud to himself. 'We always used to live in this kitchen and that's what I propose to do again.'

The walls were a light primrose yellow which made the room look sunny even on dull days. The paint was peeling and stained in places, so before bringing any of his stuff in Noël decided to get it re-decorated. He got the Yellow Pages and leafed through looking for Painters and Decorators. 'How do you tell the good ones from the cowboys?' he wondered. He hadn't hired a decorator before. Beryl had seen to all that when he was married, and a boat didn't need one. 'I'm no handyman,' he said aloud. One of his stock phrases. He heard Beth's laughter. Beth would say 'read a book about it, then do it yourself,' he thought. 'It's a huge room, but a lot of it is windows. What book? He'd have a look round the second-hand book-shops in Leeds tomorrow.

5. The Voice of the North

'What you doin' with that then?' shouted Blodwen, standing squarely in front of Noël at his desk in the newspaper office. Noël called it 'his desk' but now that he was part-time, and there was some fancy new economy thing called 'hot-desking' it was rarely his to use. Blodwen never spoke below *forte*, and when meetings got tricky her *fortissimo* was tough to deal with.

'Eating my sandwich off it,' replied Noël, resting his bacon roll on the thick volume. 'It's called the Reader's Digest Guide to doing everything for yourself, regardless of the consequences.'

'Not brain surgery I hope!' roared Blodwen. 'Ha!' Her Welsh laugh was sudden, but sincere.

'Funny you should say that,' said Noël. 'No, I'm going to decorate the kitchen.'

'Boats don't have kitchens. You could give your galley a lick round with an old toothbrush.'

'I've sold the boat,' said Noël. 'I've moved into the family acres at Treetops, just north of Ripon.'

'Oooh Posh! Too old to live on a boat now are we?'

That hurt a bit, probably because it was partly true. Blodwen could be relied on for the truth, no matter what.

'The boat's getting old too,' agreed Noël. It needs a lot of work done on it, and I'm no...' (he thought he heard a faint snicker from Beth) I'm no longer quite as bendy as I was,' he concluded. 'Fitting six feet of bloke into a narrow-boat isn't always going to be easy.'

'Better do some Keep Fit then,' blustered Blodwen and stomped off. 'Maybe keep your mouth shut sometimes girl' she thought to herself. 'He's lookin' a bit saddish. He loved that boat.'

Noël was indeed saddish. Getting home after a mediocre string quartet concert in Harrogate last night he had physically missed Archimedes. His body had learned that after the hard pavements, and the concrete quay-side, the gentle yielding of the deck as he stepped on board gave him a welcome that he'd taken for granted. There wasn't much yielding in the entrance hall at Treetops.

The next Sunday was fine, and Noël walked down to the canal. Archimedes already looked different. There were brighter curtains at the windows and a row of planters along the roof.

'That's my herb garden,' said Beth. 'Come on in.'

Hugging a mug of tea Noël told Beth his plans for the kitchen. He'd read the section on decorating and just wanted to go through it to get it clear in his mind.

'You want to do the windows first,' said Beth. 'They can be fiddly. Maybe Eddie could give you a hand.'

'Eddie's got enough to do. No – I really want to do it all myself.'

'That's good,' said Beth approvingly. 'But don't be afraid to ask. Take your time over it and enjoy it.'

'I'm going to do a bit at a time,' said Noël. 'Eating end first. Then you must come up and pass judgement.'

Beth tightened her lips as if to stop the words coming. Then she burst out 'We only just got this boat in time you know. I'm – I'm expecting!'

'Good old Archimedes!' exclaimed Noël. 'That's wonderful. I knew she'd look after things!'

The following weekend he went to visit Mike again. This time Mike's eyes focused a little quicker.

'Hi there Nole!' he said, his voice clearer than last time. 'Can we go out again?'

Noël had planned better this time and they drove out to a country pub and had proper Sunday lunch in the dining-room. Mike found it difficult to cut the beef, and the massive Yorkshire pudding defeated him entirely. At the risk of being patronising Noël had a quiet word with the waiter, who took Mike's plate away.

'He'll be back in a tick,' said Noël. 'He's just going to make it a bit easier to handle.' Mike looked a bit bewildered, but when his plate came back the beef was cut up neatly, the Yorkshire removed, and small portions of vegetables were arranged around the edge of the plate. He brightened up and managed a good half of it. It took him almost an hour and by the end he was exhausted.

As he waited for Mike to finish Noël thought about how many people must find a meal difficult to handle. How many dared not go out for fear of looking foolish or making a mess. How many old, and not so old, were trapped in an armchair waiting to die. Noël had told the waiter exactly what to do.

'Cut the meat into bite-sized pieces. Get rid of the Yorkshire. Arrange small amounts of veg in distinct spoonfuls. Make it look really attractive. Tell the chef we're enhancing his layout, not wrecking it!' All this was a long paragraph. How much easier, and less embarrassing, it would be if there was just one word. One universally accepted word among chefs that tactfully meant that someone needed help. If old people were 'a growing problem' then a universal word would be really useful. It would have to be French of course. How about 'coupée'? No 'cut' is too specific. How about 'facilitée'. Yes, 'facilitée' – made easier – could be used generally for anything from beef to meringues.

'Lobster Thermidor Facilitée, s'il vous plait,' said Noël.

'What?' said Mike.

'Nothing. Just thinking about an article for the paper,' said Noël. 'Do you fancy a pud?'

Mike's eyes glazed over. 'So tired,' he murmured.

As they left Noël gave the waiter a generous tip. 'Thanks for your help,' he whispered. 'Thanks for the Facilitée.' The waiter looked puzzled, but pleased.

Work progressed slowly at Treetops, but Noël was getting a real kick out of doing it himself. He'd done all the scraping and cleaning of the eating end. There was just the painting to do. Then he'd scrubbed the table and polished the settle so that he could work there. Hot-desking, although it sounded somehow sexy, was the last resort. He preferred to write at home in peace.

Every time he went to visit Mike he seemed a bit stronger and more alert.

'Your visits are doing him a power of good!' said Matron. 'He's beginning to take an interest in things.'

'Do you think he'd like a daily paper?' asked Noël. 'I'd be happy to arrange that.'

'We could try it,' said Matron. 'Daily might be a bit much but what about 'The Week'. That has a bit of everything in it.'

'I'll bring one next time as a try-out,' said Noël.

They always went out. The care home gave Noël the creeps, although it was a friendly place. The owners were a couple who lived on the top floor. They had a golden retriever and a black cat who roamed freely and were sociable with the residents. It couldn't be more relaxed, but what lives were locked up in those armchairs and wheelchairs? What achievements and adventures, laughter and tragedy. The wispy old professor in the corner had written a set of Latin textbooks, used all over the world. The tiny lady with bright blue eyes had been a dancer. 'Sadler's Wells you know,' she confided brightly to anyone who asked. Noël could imagine himself in one of these chairs in years to come. He could hear himself insisting to anyone who would listen 'I used to write for the papers you know. Music magazines too. I even did some entries for the New Grove Dictionary of Opera. I went out to cover the launch of the Malaysian Philharmonic Orchestra…'

And the reply would come 'Yes dear. How interesting. Did you remember to take your medication today?'

He didn't know how Mike could stand it. Nobody here probably knew what an oboe looked like, still less the soaring, heart-clutching sound that Mike made in Tchaik 4.

He began to take Mike out for longer. One day they started early and drove over to Ripon to see Archimedes. Beth, glowing with good health, gave them spiced parsnip soup and home-made flatbreads. Eddie apologised for the boat's scraped flanks.

'There's a lot of treating and filling to do before I can paint her.' Noël nodded solemnly, as one handyman to another.

Another time they went to Treetops for the day. The eating end of the kitchen was finished and they had beer and sandwiches on the scrubbed table. Noël apologised for the gloomy state of the rest of the house.

'That entrance hall needs something,' said Mike. 'Mary would have known what.'

'Maybe one of her tapestries,' said Noël. 'What happened to them?'

'They're all in the house in Manchester I think. You'll have to ask Edgar next time he's home.'

Noël filed the idea away. He'd recently seen the Quaker Tapestry at Kendal. Light and lively. Full of people doing things. Something like that would be great in the hall.

The second half of the kitchen, the business end, took much less time. Noël hung a big curtain, borrowed from Blodwen, across the room. This kept most of the dust off the eating end. He was brisker and more methodical this time and it was swiftly done. The curtain came down.

'And the curtain goes up on my completely new kitchen!' cried Noël. There was a round of applause. Some friends from the office, Beth and Eddie and Kay and Jim, from down the road, sat round the table. Corks popped, glasses clinked and spaghetti Bolognese was piled high in a big bowl.

'That's called empowerment,' said Jean sagely. She was the youngest person present and was a new recruit to the office. Unlike most of the older journalists she'd been on business training courses and was full of the new jargon.

'I call it doing things, and then feeling chuffed,' said Noël, 'but I get your drift.'

Treetops began to feel like home and nobody noticed that there wasn't a speck of meat in the spaghetti Bolognese. Beth winked at him as they left. 'Told you!' she whispered.

Months went by. The lounge at Treetops was comfortable, with an open fire and armchairs, but the only time it had been used so far was for the naming party for Beth's baby.

'We don't do christening,' said Eddie, 'but we'd like our friends to welcome her and acknowledge her name.'

The cake, and little presents, had been laid out on a table in the bay window. After the final 'Welcome Margot!' the friends had left Beth and Eddie's parents in the armchairs and gradually filtered back to the kitchen with their pieces of cake. Noël manned the punch-bowl on the range and savoured the throb of life in the house. It would be even quieter when they'd all gone, he thought. Maybe it's the moment to put on 'The Rite of Spring' at top whack.

The kitchen was now happy at both ends. The dining-room was rarely opened.

6. A trip to the South

It was spring again when Noël took Matron aside for a chat.

'I'd like to take Mike away for a weekend,' he said. 'Do you think he could cope?'

'I don't see why not. He can do most things for himself now, even though he's slow. At least he's careful. Where will you take him?'

'I don't know yet,' said Noël. 'I'd like him to choose. He isn't just a parcel after all.'

They talked about it over lunch, but it was so long since Mike had made any sort of decision that he had no ideas.

'Where did you go with Mary?' asked Noël, 'or can you remember where you went as a kid?' Mike was stumped. 'OK. Let's leave it for a bit,' said Noël. 'Something's bound to come up.'

The next time he visited Mike was as near animated as he'd ever seen him. He waved a copy of 'The Week' at Noël as he came in.

'I've got it. The Tall Ships. I'd love to see them again. I last saw them when I was down playing in the Bournemouth Orchestra.'

'When and where?' asked Noël, scanning the page.

'Next month, coming up the Solent.'

It's a hell of a long way to go for a weekend, Noël thought, but hey! Mike looks really lit up. The best solution seemed to be to book a holiday cottage for a long weekend. Then they could take all the time Mike needed to get up in the mornings. He could rest when he needed to. Noël could do meals. There was a place near Lepe which would be the perfect spot to view the ships.

They drove down one evening while the roads were quiet. Noël helped Mike to bed at about one in the morning. The next day they slept late, and then took a picnic to Lepe and had a perfect view of the stately procession. A lump came into Noël's throat as he saw Mike's eyes stretch to the horizon. It must have been years since he'd been able to look that far.

Mike straightened his shoulders, took a deep breath and said 'I could just play that Swan of Tuonela now!'

'And it would sound great!' said Noël, brushing the back of his hand across his eyes.

'Mike slept for about two days after your trip,' said Matron the next time Noël visited. 'But he's smiling and talking more.' Nevertheless Mike looked serious when Noël found him in his room.

'I've been reading about all these care homes going bust,' he said. 'It's all this new Health and Safety nonsense.'

'That's right,' said Noël. 'Something about every room having to be *en-suite*. Funny how there's no English word for *en-suite*.'

'We'd never heard of *en-suite* when I was young,' continued Mike. 'We had to wait our turn, legs crossed.'

'Is it all *en-suite* here?' asked Noël.

'Mostly. Matron was saying that about six rooms weren't, but Hugh, Violet and a few others are perfectly able to go down the corridor. Or have a you-know-what at night.'

A month later Mike looked even more serious, and Matron was nowhere to be seen.

'The owners have had to get rid of Matron,' he said as soon as he saw Noël. 'They can't afford a full-timer any more. We have some agency woman in twice a day now. The girls don't like her.'

'Let's go,' said Noël. 'I'm sure it will all settle down soon. People always hate change.'

'The dog doesn't like the new woman either,' said Mike.

They let the subject drop and drove to Nantwich for the day. A trip on the canal lifted their mood and Noël hear Mike humming the famous tune from Dvořák's 'New World'.

'Did you often get the chance to play your cor anglais?'

'Not often enough,' said Mike, 'but I used to dep for Janet Munro sometimes in the Bournemouth, and later in the CBSO. That was a treat.'

Conversations with Mike were pretty normal these days, thought Noël. He gets easily flustered, and still can't find his way around anywhere new, but things are really looking up. He smiled happily and raised his face to the warm breeze.

7. New Directions

'It's a Strategy Meeting.' It was Jean on the phone. 'The Chief wants us all there, part-timers and all.'

'What's it about?' asked Noël.

'Strategy. The Way Forward.'

'I hate military language getting into everything,' grumbled Noël. 'And who was thinking of taking the Way Backward anyway?'

'Oh you!' said Jean. 'Anyway, it's at 2 o'clock. See you then.'

Although *The Voice of the North* was published in Leeds it was no provincial rag. It covered national and international news pretty thoroughly. It was well respected for its Arts coverage and was one of the last dailies to have a children's section on Saturdays. That, and the Women's Pages, were in Blodwen's charge and were notorious for some unusual and outspoken stuff. Blodwen had twice been sacked. Once for a piece about female masturbation and once when she'd tipped a cup of tea over the sub-editor's head. Cold tea fortunately. Both times the boss had told her to leave. Both times she'd turned up as usual the next morning. There had been a loud exchange in the side-office, a loud 'Ha!' and everything had returned to normal.

Blodwen had been full-on this afternoon. Most of the meeting had been about accountability, time-management and record-keeping. Jean had taken notes and, much to Noël's relief, said she'd circulate 'hard copy' later. His mind drifted off, imagining Jean patiently chipping the Chief's words into tablets of limestone.

'Not fuckin' likely!' shouted Blodwen.

'But surely,' the Chief continued, 'most kids these days are into computer games and those pocket DS things. We're way behind the times with our Saturday Spot.'

'While there's one child alive in this kingdom…'

'Queendom,' muttered Jean.

'While there's one child who can take pleasure in the printed word,' stormed Blodwen, 'they're bloody well gettin' it.'

'But Nature Notes,' said Peter wearily 'for heaven's sake. It's so Enid Blyton.'

'It was from Enid Bloody Blyton I learned to tell a newt from a tadpole, and a lot more besides,' thundered Blodwen.

19

'The kids today – they're given these science assessment nodules – '

'Modules,' corrected Jean.

'I know what I'm sayin' girl, and I know what nodules are full of.'

The Chief raised his hand for silence. There was the sound of heavy breathing.

'So what, for example, is planned for the next Saturday Spot?' he asked as calmly as he could.

'It's on a theme,' said Blodwen, ruffling through her papers. 'Here we are. The true story of a young Ethiopian refugee, a short history of Oxfam, a quiz about famous people who helped others and a recipe. Cook some scones for your Grandma. Make the little buggers think of something beyond themselves for a change. Am I or am I not a corrupting influence?'

'Nobody said…' began the Chief. Then 'OK we'll give it another year.'

Blodwen sat down heavily, her full lips clenched. Noël sneaked a sideways look and was sure he saw a small drop shining in the corner of her eye.

'I hope it survives until Margot can read,' he thought.

As Noël left he found Peter occupying his hot-desk. 'What are you on with, Peter?' he asked.

'Some of this stuff about old folks' homes,' said Peter. 'Lots of them are closing down, or being picked up by big companies. There must be good money to be made out of the wrinklies.'

Noël winced.

'Consortiums are buying them, smartening them up, charging a fortune,' continued Peter.

'Ah. I had heard,' said Noël. 'Everything's for sale these days, even care and compassion – if you're lucky.'

'You're an old softie,' said Peter.

Old maybe, thought Noël, but I dare not go soft. Not yet. He'd not forgotten Blodwen's remark about fitness and was doing a lot more walking these days. Working part-time, and with some tips from Beth, he was cooking better meals 'mostly plants,' as it said in the Michael Pollan book she had lent him. He wouldn't say he was exactly a vegetarian as he disliked labels and 'isms'. He believed they restricted thought and invention.

His rangy figure was getting supple again after too many years of sitting at a desk. He still had a good head of hair, wavy, greying and falling forward in a way that made women want to smooth it back – or they used to, he mused. This was a good time of life. Perhaps he'd go back to learning Italian, an easy language for a musician. Maybe travel a bit more, try to pick up some of those assignments where they pay your fare, you cover a music festival and then do a favourable bit about the airline in a side-bar. When he got home he pulled out *Teach Yourself Italian* and some old travel guides and took them through to the kitchen.

8. All change

'It's happened,' said Mike. 'The owners have got to sell. They can't afford to do all those legal things.'

Noël was both sad and angry. 'It's all to do with the fear of litigation,' he growled. 'Bloody Americans started it. One old chap falls over on the way to the bog and the solicitors are in like wasps round a jam tart.'

'You can just as easily have a fall going to the *en-suite*,' said Mike. 'I've done it.'

'Funny isn't it,' said Noël. 'When you're young you 'fall over' or 'fall down'. When you're old you 'have a fall'. It's as if it is something ominous that's done to old people. Of course it can be serious if you break something, but so can it when you're young.'

'Got to die of something when you're old,' said Mike cheerfully. 'Let's get out and have some air.'

They had planned to make a weekend of it and stay at Treetops. There was a concert at Leeds Town Hall, a visiting orchestra from Germany. Noël thought he'd risk taking Mike. Going to hear an orchestra was something they hadn't tried yet and Noël was apprehensive that it might upset Mike. His humming might be a problem too, so Noël had been to see the manager and explained the difficulty.

'I don't think it will be a sell-out,' said the manager. 'They're playing Messiaen in the second half. It frightens the natives! I'll reserve you a place in the gallery, and keep some of the seats empty around it.' As it turned out Noël needn't have worried. Mike was alert and focused all through, and not a hum passed his lips. At the end he was exhausted and Noël had to help him down the stairs. When they got back to Treetops Noël asked cautiously 'Was that OK then – the concert?'

'Overture too fast. First trumpet a bit sharp, Messiaen bloody marvellous,' said Mike.

'Nothing much wrong with that bit of his brain then,' thought Noël. To make things easier for Mike Noël had put a bed into the dining-room. It was next to the downstairs cloakroom. The mahogany staircase had wide shiny banisters that weren't easy to hold, and stairs were always a problem for Mike's weaker left leg.

That night Noël wrote his piece about the concert ('Overture a little hasty, intonation in the brass section not always reliable, Messiaen a tour-de-force....') and emailed it in. As he went upstairs he could hear Mike snoring softly. It was rather comforting having someone else in the place.

It was a few weeks before Noël got over to see Mike again. The Chief had decided on a bold new venture and he wanted Noël involved. There was another Strategy Meeting.

'The Environment,' announced the Chief. There was silence. 'Climate Change. Global Warming,' he went on.

Peter sighed, turned sideways in his chair and crossed his long legs. 'What about it Chief?'

'Things are happening. People are worried.'

'Things have always happened and people have always been worried,' said Peter. 'That's how the government keeps them under control – always some background fear going on. We need some real solid science behind global warming before sticking our necks out.'

'None of the mainstream media are giving it much prominence,' continued the Chief, 'but there's plenty of solid evidence worldwide. The oil companies hate it of course and put billions into lobbying and misinformation.'

'What do you suggest we do?' asked Noël.

''I want an Eco-Page every weekend,' said the Chief. 'Just a page to start with, maybe going to a full pull-out section later.'

'Bloody Great!' roared Blodwen. 'Put it next the kids' page. It's them who'll be needin' the know-how to clear up the friggin' mess we've left them.'

It was one of the liveliest meetings they'd ever had. Each of them took on a different aspect to research and another meeting was called for the following week.

'He's a fool,' said Peter quietly to Noël as they left the meeting. 'It's like those predictions that the world will end on a certain date – it will all fizzle out. New technologies will take over and solve the problems. That's what always happens.'

'He's certainly brave,' said Noël. 'Other papers do the odd feature, but most really bad environmental news is given a small para on an inside page. We mustn't frighten people too much or they might stop spending!'

Noël's remit was to expand his book reviews to bring in more on environmental subjects, and DVDs as well. 'I'll ask Eddie,' he thought. 'He'll have some good ideas.'

July was unusually fine and Noël planned to take Mike out to Hare Hill in Cheshire. There were gardens and shady woodland with a walk through to Alderley Edge. Too far for Mike to walk, but the National Trust had electric buggies for hire. As he came in through the door of the care home he noticed a desk had been placed in one corner of the entrance hall. A young woman looked at him over her glasses.

'Can I help you?'

'I've come to take Mike out,' said Noël.

She ran her finger down a list. 'Would that be Mr Michael Powell or Mr Michael Dobson?' she enquired.'

'Mike Powell,' said Noël.

'I can see no record of your request here,' she said. 'When did you send it in?'

'Since when have you needed a request?' said Noël irritably. 'I usually just come over when I can.'

'Yes I'm afraid things were rather lax under the previous ownership,' she replied, pursing her lips. 'We have to be very careful these days you know. Are you a relative?'

'No, but Mike knows me well enough,' said Noël. 'Won't that do?'

'He does have some cognitive problems however,' she replied severely.

'I know his short-term memory is a bit unreliable, and he gets lost easily,' said Noël, 'but I'm long-term. He's known me for over twenty-five years.'

She rose reluctantly and came round the desk. 'We'll just go through to the lounge. What's your name please? Mine is Miss Blain.'

'Noël Burke,' said Noël, perhaps rather too clearly. Mustn't get ratty, he told himself. They might take it out on Mike.

'Please say nothing more,' said Miss Blain. They went through to the lounge where Mike could be seen reading. Noël saw with delight that it was a book, not just a newspaper. His concentration must be improving. He was about to comment on this when Miss Blain laid her hand on his arm. At that moment Mike looked up.

'Hi there Nole! Who's the girlfriend? About time too!'

Miss Blain stepped hastily aside. 'Now Mr Powell' she said solemnly. 'You know me. I'm the new secretary.'

'Never seen you before,' said Mike confidently. 'Can we go out Nole?'

'Mr Burke just has to fill out a form, Mr Powell, then you can go.'

'Mr Burke?' laughed Mike. 'We all used to call him Noley. Sometimes Holy Noley if he wrote a good review.'

Back at the desk Noël was given a four-page form. 'No need to do it all,' conceded Miss Blain. 'Your name and full details here, proposed time of departure and return here. Mobile phone number here. Then a brief description of the destination and purpose of your outing, including any activities that might be thought risky for Mr Powell. You then sign as taking full responsibility here. Fortunately the CRB check isn't, as yet, mandatory.'

Noël wrote quickly while Miss Blain helped Mike to zip up his jacket. Then he folded the form and slapped the pen down on it.

'OK let's go. See you later.'

'What was all that stuff you had to write?' asked Mike as they drove off.

'Oh just that we were going white-water rafting, then doing a bungee jump off Clifton Suspension Bridge – and that I was fully responsible for you.'

'We're not are we?' gasped Mike. He began to tremble.

'Course not!' said Noël. 'A trundle round some golden woodlands followed by stately home tea and buns.'

'Phew!' said Mike. 'You had me worried.' Noël reminded himself to be a bit more careful in future. It was one thing to give Miss Blain the frights, but Mike's slower speed of comprehension meant that he didn't always spot a joke.

When they returned, and Mike was safely in his armchair (how Noël hated that armchair) Miss Blain took him aside.

'Now a joke is a joke, Mr Burke, and I can see your friendship with Mr Powell is genuine. In future however please be more careful what you write on our forms. Humour isn't a strong point with our management, and patient safety is paramount.'

'Sorry. I just couldn't resist it. I hate all this bureaucracy coming between people. And Mike isn't a 'patient', he's a resident. He isn't ill.'

'I've put you down on our list of approved visitors for Mr Powell,' continued Miss Blain, 'but advance notice is essential.'

'Sometimes I don't know until the last minute,' said Noël. 'My work is a bit unpredictable. Would an e-mail do?'

'Yes, that would be acceptable.' She picked up a smart business card. 'Here's the address, and Mr Powell is resident number...' she consulted her list, '5048, which you should quote. I'll write it on the card for you. It all goes through our central database you see.'

Noël felt slightly sick as he drove home. He felt that a barrier had been erected between him and Mike. Their friendship had been tainted by doubt and the need for proof of honesty. Did the girls have to call him 'Mr Powell' too, he wondered. Rosa, the one from Romania, always gave Mike a big hug when she came on duty. I bet that's forbidden now, he thought.

That night he had a dream. He was in an armchair in the care home with all the others. He couldn't move his legs. Mike was in his usual place by the window. Noël tried to call out to him 'I'm here too Mike,' but no sound came. Then Mike slowly turned his head towards him and Noël saw that he had no eyes.

'No!' he shouted himself awake. He was shaking and sweating. He got up for a pee, then went down to the kitchen and put the kettle on. He pulled a pad towards him and began to write: 'Dear Edgar...'

26

9. More change

It was all sorted by Christmas. The dining-table, chairs and sideboard had been sold to a dealer who specialised in mahogany. He had also stripped out the panelling and quoted Noël a price way below its value. The naked plaster of the dining-room didn't daunt Noël as much as it might have done earlier. He gratefully accepted help from Eddie as time was short. Jim from down the road came and gave a hand. His wife made new curtains and the heavy old brocade ones went off to the local theatre club to be made into costumes. By early December the room was transformed. They had even managed to squeeze a small '*en- suite*' into one corner – just a lavatory and a tiny hand-basin. Nobody had yet found an English word for it. When Mike heard about the drilling and excavation he'd called it 'Nole's Poo Hole.'

Noël had found a painting of the Tall Ships. Beth had made a patchwork quilt for the bed with glowing colours. A suitable chair for Mike had been a problem. Most armchairs 'for the elderly' gave Noël the creeps. In the end they found a beautifully crafted rocking-chair, with soft leather padding and an ingenious locking device so that it didn't rock when you didn't want it to. Getting in and out was made easier by a separate gadget which tipped it forward a little.

'Stunning design, made in Cornwall by a mad inventor bloke,' said Eddie, who had found it in one of his Eco-magazines. 'Doesn't use power like those posh recliners, and isn't so bulky either.' Beth made a couple of cushions for it in the same patchwork colours as the bedspread.

Edgar had a week's leave from his job in Nigeria. As he had power of attorney he had to sign off all the paperwork at the care home. He also set up a standing order to Noël for Mike's share of household expenses.

'He can probably run his own current account now,' said Noël. 'He's found a good way of remembering his PIN anyway!'

As he drove over to fetch Mike, the last time he'd ever have to make that journey, he shuddered as he remembered his previous visit. After the nightmare, and the drafting of the letter to Edgar, he'd gone back to see Mike pretty soon, 'before Miss Blain forgets me,' he'd thought.' At the front desk was a burly man with a shaven head and a military sweater. He'd looked at Noël suspiciously.

'Name?' he barked.

'Noël Burke. I'm on the visitors' list for Mike Powell. Is Miss Blain off duty this weekend?'

'Off sick. 'Flu. Identification?'

'Oh. Right.' Noël felt in his pockets. 'Will this do?' He produced his Leeds City Council parking permit.

'Need two. Full security.'

Noël found his press pass, which usually worked wonders. He saw the man twitch.

'OK. In you go.'

Noël had found Mike in his usual place by the window. He was reading 'A Time of Gifts'.

'Powerful writer this chap,' said Mike. 'I wish I'd travelled more when I was young. Couldn't afford it though.'

'Nor me,' said Noël.

'Where are we going today then?' Mike closed the book, using a strip of newspaper as a book-mark.

'No time for an outing I'm afraid,' said Noël. 'I just popped over to put an idea to you. Can we go somewhere private?

'We can go to my room.' Mike hauled himself up. 'What's the big secret? Got a girl at last?'

Noël took his arm. Over his shoulder he saw the security guard watching them. Once they were settled he outlined his plan, ending by summing it all up to make sure Mike had taken it in.

'You're so much fitter now. My house is far too big for just me. We enjoy each other's company, but there's space for privacy. This place is getting more like a prison every day…' he tailed off. Mike shook his head. 'Take some time to think about it,' Noël went on. 'I'll come back next week.' Mike shook his head again then rubbed his eyes and ears as if trying to get rid of cobwebs.

'I can't believe it,' he said slowly. Hey Noley… what a… what a… what a plan!'

'I've written this letter to Edgar, hoping you'd say yes,' went on Noël. 'Will you read it to see if it's OK?'

Mike read the letter slowly. He put it down. Then he picked it up and read it again. Noël held his breath. Mike raised his head and looked straight into Noël's eyes.

'How soon can I get out?'

'Left him in his room have you?' said the guard as Noël made for the front door.

'Yes, he's having a quiet read.'

'Pretty quiet place all round,' said the guard. 'Much rougher where I usually work.'

'Where's that?'

'Liverpool. Two big care homes over there. Security can be a major headache.'

'Really?' Noël was itching to go, but sensed the guard wanted to talk. If people know you're from the press they usually want to tell you stuff.

'I could tell you a thing or two,' said the guard, warming to his subject. Noël shifted from one foot to the other. 'One old bloke used to get took out by his "nephew".' That word 'nephew' came with a health warning, thought Noël.

'And?'

'Every time he came back he was quieter,' said the guard. 'Then began to be sick every time.' He paused for dramatic effect.

'Was his nephew trying to poison him to get his inheritance?'

'No. Worse. They analysed his sick. D'you know what was in it?'

'Can't imagine.'

'Sperm. Lots of it!' said the guard triumphantly. 'Nephew – and company…'

'Oh God!'

'And then there was this upper-class lady,' went on the guard. 'They always choose the posh ones – they won't talk…'

'Sorry,' said Noël. 'Maybe you can save it for next time. I've got to go.'

'Oke!' said the guard. 'I'll just go and check Mr Powell. Can't be too careful.'

Noël ran across the car-park and slammed the car into gear.

'No bloody next time!' he screamed as he skidded across the gravel.

10. Moving in

The next Strategy Meeting was buzzing. Blodwen had been round several local Primary Schools, terrifying the head teachers. She had a list of questions about school dinners and what was happening in the school grounds. A lucky few were cooking with organic or local produce, one had photo-voltaic panels on the roof and the children were making a daily graph of how many kilowatts they were generating. This was to be given a high star rating on the first Eco-Page. Noël had reviewed half a dozen books, including *Blessed Unrest* in which Paul Hawken had a list 100 pages long of organisations 'working towards ecological sustainability and social justice.' Hawken reckoned the total was more than a million, maybe nearer two.

Peter had been visiting some of the big businesses in Leeds to get their views, many of which were unprintable. Jean was in the early stages of setting up a new section of the website for the Eco-Pages where there would be an archive section with useful links.

'We'll connect the site to all the social media when we're up and running,' she said confidently. Noël wondered where there was a dictionary of modern jargon he could consult.

'We go live in the New Year,' said the Chief. 'Short notice I know, but I'd like us to be the first paper brave enough to tackle this.'

Peter shook his head. 'They'll think we've gone all beards and sandals,' he sighed.

'Well that's bloody out of date!' shouted Blodwen. 'That Attenborough bloke talks about Climate Change, and he's a Sir. Wears proper shoes too.'

Noël was more cheerful than he'd ever felt after one of the Chief's sessions. He perched on the corner of Blodwen's desk.

'Guess what?' he said happily. 'Mike's leaving that terrible care home in Manchester and coming to live with me at Treetops.'

There was an uncharacteristic silence next to him. He turned to look at Blodwen and she was looking at him thoughtfully. They all knew about Mike of course, they had done for years. His superb playing had often been mentioned in reviews. They had followed his fortunes on and off during coffee breaks. They had heard about the take-over at the care home. It had linked in to the series Peter was working on called 'Public and Private'. Blodwen spoke again.

'What?' said Noël. He'd never experienced Blodwen's *pianissimo* before and had his ears turned down.

'I said you haven't gone bloody gay have you?' she roared. Papers were put down on desks, or in some cases lifted up as a shield. You could hear many pairs of ears twitching.

Noël roared with laughter.

'What do *you* think?' he challenged her, and leaned over to kiss her plump cheek.

'Oh 'ell. Sorry,' said Blodwen. 'Put my effin' foot in it again.'

'It's OK Blod,' said Noël. 'If I was I wouldn't mind, but as I'm not I don't either.'

She puzzled over this for a while, then

'Ha!'

It was all over.

Jean touched his sleeve as he passed her desk. 'Won't it restrict your personal mobility?' she asked. 'You were planning to travel more now you're part-time, weren't you?'

'Oh I'm sure we can travel, both of us,' said Noël, touched by her concern. 'We'll just go slower, that's all. He isn't actually ill you know.'

'Good,' said Jean. 'I'm sure you've considered all the possible consequences before taking this decision.'

Not sure that I've considered anything much, said Noël to himself. My guts just tell me it's the right thing to do. I wish I could offer a home to all the old dears. He replayed all these scenes as he made the final journey to Manchester, sometimes laughing, sometimes groaning.

Mike was in the hall with a small suitcase. The rest of his belongings were coming in a Transit van the next day. There wasn't much, just the contents of his room, but he had a small upright piano, which couldn't fit in Noël's car. Noël chatted cheerfully on the way home, doing imitations of Blodwen which always made Mike laugh. Suddenly he realised that Mike had gone quiet, so he said no more, thinking he must have nodded off. He glanced to his left and saw that Mike was shuddering, and his face had a fixed stare.

31

'You OK Mike?' he asked anxiously. When there was no reply his stomach clenched. He pulled in to the next lay-by.

'Mike,' he said gently. 'What's up?'

Mike gradually turned towards him. Noël had a flashback to his nightmare, but the eyes were there. Oh thank God. They gradually focused and Mike's tension relaxed.

'Sorry Nole,' he said eventually. 'I suddenly got scared. I've been in that place too bloody long. Couldn't wait to get out, but – it was sort-of safe.'

'Of course. I should have realised,' said Noël. 'I haven't been thinking clearly. Too pleased with my great plan to consider the side-effects.'

'It's OK,' said Mike. 'Keep driving. I've got over that panic attack. I used to get them a lot after the stroke. Not so much now.'

'I suppose our outings were so well-spaced and gradual that it didn't happen before,' said Noël.

'That's right. That bungee jump idea nearly did it though!'

Noël made several mental notes to himself, and drove on.

11. Christmas

Mike's room was a great success. The piano fitted in. Books and CDs went into a tall bookshelf on the opposite wall. The chair took a bit of getting used to, but once Mike got the hang of the locking device it was perfect. One of Mary's tapestries hung on the wall above a small desk where he could keep his personal papers and a laptop. Not that he used the laptop at all. It had been Mary's, and he'd never got the hang of it.

'Looks good though,' he grinned. 'I like to feel up-to-date.'

'You could use it to watch television,' said Noël, 'as I haven't got one.'

'Maybe,' said Mike vaguely.

Christmas was a quiet affair this year. Beth, Eddie and Margot stayed on the boat, which they had decorated with green branches and hundreds of tiny white solar lights.

'If the sun shines it looks like fairyland at night,' said Beth. 'Margot loves it, and I want her first real Christmas to be on the boat. Anyway,' she added, 'I'm expecting again. I keep throwing up. Not very sociable.'

Blodwen had gone to Wales. 'Land of my Bloody Father's,' she'd bellowed. 'And my Mother's, and the flippin' Aunties.'

Jean was going to York. 'I'm staying with my significant other,' she said cryptically. Nobody knew where Peter went. Someone had seen him with his wife once, but he never talked about his personal life. Maybe she wasn't his wife. In answer to a direct question about Christmas he'd said 'Oh I expect we'll play it by ear,' then, with a sigh, 'as usual.'

Kay and Jim invited them for elevenses on Christmas Day, which involved Buck's Fizz. Mike had managed with his stick and Noël's arm to walk all the way down to their house, but Jim had to give them a lift back home. Then Mike had a snooze while Noël cooked the lunch.

'I'm afraid it will be a meatless Christmas,' he'd warned Mike. 'I've just reviewed a documentary DVD called 'Food Inc'. It's all about where food comes from and how it's processed.'

'Grim was it?' asked Mike.

'Almost pushed me over the edge,' said Noël. 'We might have the odd anchovy though.'

'Suits me,' said Mike. He wasn't a fussy eater. 'Don't anchovies have feelings then?'

'Aaaargh! Don't ask me that!'

After dinner they actually went into the lounge.

'Didn't know you had one,' said Mike, looking around. There was no Christmas tree in the bay window, but a good blaze in the fireplace. Noël got out the brandy and his grandfather's cut-glass goblets.

'This is OK,' said Noël as he leaned back and stretched out his legs.

'This is OK,' said Mike.

12. Another year

Life at Treetops settled into a sort of rhythm, but there were a few hiccups to begin with. A couple of days after Christmas Mike came into the kitchen and stood there shaking.

'I'll have to go back,' he said.

Noël dropped the toast he was buttering.

'What's up? What's happened?'

'I can't stay. I don't *know* you,' said Mike, and the trembling got faster.

'Here, sit down,' said Noël, pulling a chair forward. 'We'll talk about it.' He brought a chair up beside Mike and waited. He didn't know what to say. What Mike said had hurt, and to be honest he felt angry. No that wasn't right. You can't be angry with someone who was shaking like that.

'I'll make some tea,' he said in the end. He had to do something. While he stood by the kettle he watched Mike's back. To his relief the shuddering slowed and eventually stopped. Mike drew a deep breath, then leaned forward, put his arms on the table and rested his head on his hands.

'Here. Cup of char,' said Noël. 'Not very strong, but I've put a bit of sugar in.'

Mike straightened up. 'God! That's better,' he said. 'I think I must have had one of those panic attacks.'

'I think you did,' said Noël. 'Scared me a bit too. What triggered it?'

'No idea. Maybe just all the new experiences.'

'Well let's hope your system settles down in a while. Here – try the tea.'

While Mike drank the tea, apparently quite normally, Noël went into the hall and opened the front door. The cold air was welcome and he stepped outside. 'Ouch! That was painful,' he said to himself. I must be ready for it next time. There were a few next times, but no matter how Noël had prepared himself the words 'I don't *know* you' cut like a blunt blade. Not deep, but bruising. Mercifully these attacks became increasingly rare as Mike settled in to his new life. Noël was learning too – how to pace things. Always thinking ahead.

Each morning he would take Mike his breakfast on a tray. Mike would spend a couple of hours at least listening to the radio, putting his socks on, drinking his tea, stopping everything if certain pieces of music were played.

'That Classic FM,' he grumbled. 'They sell their Smooth Classics like brands of face-cream. Then the fast stuff is always too fast and hyped up. As for the adverts….'

'It's not meant for musicians,' laughed Noël. 'It's for Music Lovers. Different breed altogether.'

'That' true,' said Mike.

'People find that difficult to understand. They can see the difference between an artist and an art lover, but the mentality of a practising musician isn't easily explained.'

Mike nodded.

'Can't find words to explain music,' he said quietly. 'That's the whole point of it.'

While Mike spent the morning listening, humming and gradually getting dressed, Noël could get the chores done. If he had to go in to the office he tried to go in the mornings. Mike didn't mind being left alone for an hour or two.

One day Noël got back to hear Mike on the phone.

'Sorry, can't help you there. I just can't remember. I'll have to ring you back.'

'Hi Mike. It's me. What can't you remember?'

'My PIN,' said Mike, putting the phone down. 'That was the bank, checking my account details. Couldn't remember the PIN though I know it's to do with a piece of music.'

Noël hummed a few bars of Tchaikovsky.

'Ah got it! 1812!'

'Mike listen,' said Noël urgently. Mike was still humming.

'Kept thinking of other pieces. 633 Squadron. Pacific 231 – not enough numbers. I must ring back.'

Noël put his hands on Mike's shoulders. 'Listen, listen, listen!'

'What?' Mike looked alarmed.

'Never ever, *ever* give your PIN to anybody.'

'Not even the bank?'

'That wasn't the bank on the phone. It was some crook trying to get into your account.'

'Oh Lor! Are you sure?'

'Quite sure. It's a common trick. Have you ever had a call like that before, and given them your number?'

'No, never,' said Mike.

Noël wondered though, as Mike's short-term memory played strange tricks. Some things he remembered clearly, others just vanished.

'To be safe let's go down to town and change the number. We can check your account too and see if anything's been taken out.'

'The phone rang three times this morning,' said Mike. 'Two were just silent – nobody there.'

'Those would be nuisance calls too. They dial a load of numbers automatically, then talk to the first person who picks up. Usually trying to sell you something.'

'I don't like it,' said Mike. 'It's frightening.' He began to shake. Noël thought quickly.

'It's probably best if you don't answer the phone at all when I'm out. If it's someone we know they will try again or leave a message.'

'What if it's you?' said Mike, 'telling me you'll be late or something.'

'We'll get you a mobile,' said Noël. 'Something simple with just my number on, and Beth and Eddie's, Kay and Jim's. You won't get nuisance calls on that.' Not yet anyway, he added to himself grimly. Again he fumed inwardly at the way the elderly were being exploited.

Jean did some online research and found the ideal mobile for Mike.

'You can keep it on the windowsill and it will charge up by sunlight while you're getting dressed,' explained Noël.

'What if it's cloudy?'

'There's a charging cable too. I've put just three numbers in. Press green and then One. That's me. Green and Two is Beth, Green and Three is Jim. When the call's finished you press Red, for Stop.' It took several days for Mike to learn all this, but eventually he was pretty confident.

'That phone is perfect,' Noël told Jean next time he was in the office. 'Thanks so much for finding it.'

Jean looked at him thoughtfully. 'Mike's a bit more life-challenging than you expected isn't he?'

'Oh we get along fine,' said Noël lightly. 'Problems turn up, but there's usually a solution.'

'Are you getting away this year?'

'Yes, we're going to France for a couple of weeks. Something easy to start with.'

'Where will you go?'

'I've booked a cottage on the Ile de Ré. We'll go by train all the way. Easy!'

'Good luck!' said Jean.

Later that month, when they drove down to Sussex to visit Noël's mother and sister, they stopped for a coffee at a service area. Mike needed the Gents. As it was clearly visible from where they were sitting Noël pointed him in the right direction, rather than accompanying him. This was part of his plan to build Mike's confidence.

'It's that blue door,' said Noël, 'and when you come out you'll see me here. I won't move.' This initiative-building is going well, thought Noël. I'm getting him to choose where we go, when we stop. It's too easy to just decide everything for him. Ten minutes later there was no sign of Mike. Reluctantly Noël went to look for him, not wanting to treat him as a child. There was no sign of him in the Gents. Then Noël saw that there was another exit, to the outside. He rushed out and looked both ways. No sign of Mike. Feeling sick Noël pounded round the building and back in through the front again. Round the shop and café, back through the Gents. Still no sign. Then he tried the car-park and there was Mike, leaning comfortably against a Dormobile enjoying the sunshine.

'There you are!' gasped Noël. Then with an effort to sound calm, 'sorry it took a while to find you.'

'That's OK,' said Mike. 'I thought you were a bit long at the Poo Hole, but these things can't be rushed.'

No it wasn't *me* at the Gents, it was *you*, Noël wanted to shout, but he bit his lip. Unless it was something really significant there was no point in correcting all Mike's muddles. It only undermined his confidence.

'You're quite right,' said Noël. 'It's my age you know! Let's go.'

As they drove on Noël began to wonder: am I living his life, or is he living mine? Maybe it doesn't matter much. The alternative is unthinkable.

13. About music

It was very strange that one of the things that sometimes came between Noël and Mike was the very thing that had brought them together – music. Mike loved to listen, all day if nothing else was going on. It was usually Classic FM, although much about it irritated him.

'Trouble with Radio 3,' he said, 'if you don't time it right you get these beard-stroking academics binding on.'

'Know what you mean,' said Noël, 'but the sound quality is much better, and you get whole works played through.'

'I need to mark up the Radio Times,' said Mike, but he always forgot.

Noël, as he'd explained to Eddie, preferred live music and rarely listened to anything else, unless there was a reason, or some happy chance. Another problem was the humming. Mike either hummed along with bits he knew or, sometimes – and more disturbingly – hummed something completely different. Noël liked his music uninterrupted and 'straight to the bloodstream' as he put it. Interruptions drove him mad. This led to the third, more difficult problem.

'This is the Minuet and Trio,' informed Mike sagely in the middle of Mozart's Symphony No.39.

'Er – yes. Why are you telling me this?' enquired Noël.

'Well it's part of the traditional structure of 18th Century classical symphonic form.' Mike had slipped into teacher mode. Now I could take this as an insult to my musical intelligence, thought Noël carefully, or I could just think of it as another interruption. Either way it wound him up, so he would often quietly leave the room and maybe stand outside the front door for a few minutes. The very hardest part of all was if, when he got back, Mike said something on the lines of:

'Pity you don't seem to like Mozart. He was a very talented composer you know.' Worse still was 'You do *like* music don't you? I hope so. It means a lot to me.'

Like the 'I don't *know* you,' episodes this hurt in a very deep and painful way for which Noël, with all his writing talent, could not find adequate words. After one particularly trying episode Noël went to talk to Cecil about it.

'That's a difficult one' said Cecil. 'Let me think about it. You don't want to hurt his feelings but you don't want yours hurt either.'

The next time they met Cecil gave him a wink.

'I think I've found a bearable antidote to your problem,' he said. 'Asserting or defending your musicianship won't work, and would sound odd and false.'

'Like "the more he proclaimed his honesty the faster we counted the spoons"' said Noël.

'Exactly. Next time it happens you could say something like "That's one of your absolute favourites isn't it? Let me play you one of mine." And then put on just one movement of something you love. Forgive it for not being live. A bit of Brahms or Mendelssohn could move the situation on nicely for both of you.'

'I'll try that,' said Noël. 'A bit of Mendelssohn Octet can work wonders at most times. I'll keep it handy!'

Noël had immense respect for Cecil. He was someone who always listened with full attention and could be relied on for thoughtful answers.

It was after covering the York Early Music Festival that Noël first met Cecil and Emily. Noël had been writing a daily piece for *The Voice of the North*. One night he got back to Archimedes very late and completed his report hastily. There had been three concerts that day and he was tired out. On the drive back to Ripon he'd worked out his angle and the piece was done and sent off by about 1.30 am.

A few days later he received an unusual and beautiful letter. The black italic script formed a decorative panel in the centre of the smooth cream paper and was signed modestly 'yours in friendship Cecil Richardson'. The letter pointed out very gently and circumspectly that Jean Titelouze was not a native of Rouen, although he was the organist at the cathedral, but was born in St. Omer. Also that he was born in 1652/3 not 1650. The letter was pure joy to receive and made Noël want to meet its author. He knew that he could not write anything so elegant in reply, so decided to telephone his thanks and apologies.

Cecil's voice was softly modulated and welcoming. He told Noël that he'd always been interested in music of the Renaissance and Baroque. Now that he was retired he was using his time to build a collection of specialised books and recordings of the period. He had also just acquired an exquisite harpsichord made by a local craftsman. Might Noël like to come and see it?

From the moment that Noël entered The Crow's Nest, which overlooked the Ouse south of York, he felt at home. Cecil and Emily were Quakers and lived in this retreat house where people could come to stay if they needed some time of peace.

'People can stay for several days, up to a week,' explained Emily, 'but usually that's all they need. The charges are very reasonable and three simple meals a day are provided. Visitors don't have to be Quakers – anybody can come.'

'It must mean a lot of work for you,' said Noël. Cecil and Emily both appeared to be well into their seventies.

'The cottage next door is also Quaker property,' said Emily. 'The young couple who live there do most of the work. We're just here if needed. Pastoral care I suppose you'd call it, or as house parents.'

'We took it on when we retired from teaching,' said Cecil. 'We were in a Quaker boarding school. I taught music and Emily taught Spanish and French. We're used to being house parents.'

Noël became very fond of the Richardsons, and they of him. They showed a great interest in Mike too, and Cecil added Mike's recording of the Albinoni Concertos to his collection.

14. Noël and Beryl

After rather a staid upbringing at Treetops, and attending Ripon Grammar School, Noël had won a scholarship to the Royal College of Music. His first study was piano, and he also played the oboe. London was quite a challenge to the tall, rather reserved Northern lad. He took his studies seriously and his first year was spent exploring the capital city, mostly on foot, and going to concerts as often as he could afford to. For his own benefit he usually wrote reviews of the concerts and filed them away for future reference.

Once, during a piano lesson, his tutor had mentioned the pianist Leonard Kraus.

'Oh yes. I heard him earlier this year,' said Noël. 'There was something about his playing that made me uneasy, but I can't quite remember what. I must look up my notes.'

His tutor asked him to bring the notes to his next lesson and was impressed by Noël's file. There were newspaper reports inserted alongside his own reports, and he was often amused by their similarities and, more often, by their differences.

'May I borrow this file for a week?' asked his tutor. 'I know someone who might be interested.'

The 'someone' turned out to be the editor of a well-known music magazine, and this was how Noël's career in music journalism began. When he left the RCM he did some freelance work as a piano accompanist, and occasionally as an oboist in one of the many orchestras that flourished in London at that time. Increasingly however his time was taken up with writing and he had little time to keep up his practice.

'Life just seemed to sort itself out rather conveniently,' he told Mike when they first started talking about their personal lives.

'Apart from Beryl,' commented Mike. 'Tell me about Beryl.'

'Beryl was an art student at the Royal College of Art. Beryl was fun. Beryl painted abstracts that zinged off the wall. Beryl laughed a lot and that was what I really needed in those days. I was horribly serious.'

'Did you know about sex?' asked Mike.

'Not really, but Beryl did. She saw me as a blank canvas. She took it upon herself to light my inner fire!'

'Blimey!' said Mike. 'Was it good?'

'It was intoxicating, breath-taking and rather terrifying.'

'And?'

'It did nothing for my oboe playing.'

'I see. Good thing too. You might have got the Hallé job. Then where would I be?'

'Not a chance! I was never in your league. Semi-pro for a short time and that was it.'

'So what happened next?'

'A predictable story really. Too much sex and excitement. Pregnancy. Marriage. Miscarriage. I wasn't much fun any more. I'd wanted the baby more than Beryl did. Arguments. Going our own ways. Beryl finds a more exciting bloke. Divorce.'

'How long did all that take?'

'Ten years. Ten lost bloody years.'

'No kids then?'

'Nope.'

'Anyone else special?'

'Just one. A cellist. I'll tell you about her another time, when I'm not feeling so Berylled.'

'Sad story?'

'Wonderful, but eventually very sad indeed. I've got a hell of a lot of good friends though.' Noël clapped Mike on the shoulder.

'Much safer.'

'Much.'

15. Kay and Jim

Jim had been a colleague of Noël's father at the University, and he and Kay lived down the hill from Treetops towards town. Jim's subject was economics.

'I was still using text-books from the previous century,' he laughed, 'until my last few years.'

'What happened?' asked Noël, as he sipped Kay's excellent hot chocolate one cold morning.

'I started reading some radical stuff, starting gently with Schumacher 'Small is Beautiful' and 'The Limits to Growth' published by the Club of Rome. Then Buddhist and Green economics as the world financial systems began to creak at the joints. Then Herman Daly on Steady State Economics – it was like being born again!'

'Did you alter your teaching?' asked Noël.

'I had to go carefully. I tried introducing a bit of critical commentary into my lectures, but it was difficult to shake the pattern of thinking of the last 200 years without getting into trouble with the authorities. Then came the 2008 crash, reliably predicted by many green economists, but apparently not by mainstream financiers. The Queen was right to be puzzled that none of them expected it!'

'You must meet Peter at *The Voice of the North* ,' said Noël. 'He's meant to be researching the business aspect of our weekly Eco-Page, but he's struggling to get much that's positive out of Corporate Leeds.'

'Glad to,' said Jim. 'Maybe Kay could contribute too. We'll be needing her talents when we're having to make our own clothes again!'

16. Learning from Cecil and Emily

The daffodils were out beneath the pines at Treetops. The rain which had fallen for about a fortnight had stopped at last and the sun had some warmth in it. The front door stood open, letting welcome light into the panelled hall.

Noël squelched across the lawn and looked down at the river's curve, edged with the tall terraces of Ure Bank. The fields were full of water and the river almost touched the tops of the arches of the old bridge. Not that you could see that from here, thought Noël. Good old Great-Grandfather, choosing to build on high land. Noël had rung the Richardsons to ask how the Ouse at York was, as it was famous for flooding.

'We're high enough here,' said Emily, 'but it's pretty bad in the city. We've got an elderly couple staying here for a week while their son gets their basement pumped out.'

'How's Cecil?'

'He's away staying with his sister Lily over in Cheshire,' said Emily. 'She's got Alzheimer's and his other sister Anna looks after her. Cecil gives her a week's break every few months.'

'That's good of him'

'There's a daily help who comes in to do the housework and cooking. Cecil keeps Lily company and takes her out each day.'

Noël thought about all the families who couldn't afford help. Who had no obliging relatives. Hundreds and thousands of aging people shut in alone, going quietly mad.

'Cecil is amazing with her,' went on Emily. 'Lily keeps asking the same few questions over and over again. Cecil finds a different and interesting response every time.'

'What does she ask?'

'Where's Mummy? When can I go home? Things like that. If Cecil plays the piano to her though she is quiet and happy.'

'That's interesting,' said Noël.

'He gets a lot of practice done! I've heard that response to music is the very last thing to leave you when you have Alzheimer's.'

'Music does much more for people than anyone realises,' said Noël. 'Yet governments happily drop it from the curriculum when savings are to be made. I went and interviewed an MP about it once.'

'Oh yes. What did he say?'

'He was very gracious. Invited me to coffee on the terrace of the Houses of Parliament. Agreed with me wholeheartedly.'

'But?'

'But he said that unfortunately Labour thinks the arts are worthy, and the Conservatives think the arts are worthy but boring. His very words.'

17. On Holiday

'Train to London. Overnight in Bloomsbury. Train to Paris. Change stations. Train to La Rochelle. Taxi across the bridge to the Ile de Ré and into 'Le Petit Chevrier' by teatime.'

'That's a piece by Tomasi,' said Mike. 'Tricky one for oboe. It's meant to be for flute.'

'It's the name of our cottage at St. Martin on the Ile de Ré.'

The journey was surprisingly easy. They got a wheelchair at St. Pancras and another waited for them at the Gare du Nord. The taxi over-charged, but hey, it's France! Mike slept in an armchair while Noël unpacked. They had travelled light, as journalists know well how to do. They had supper at a restaurant on the quay watching the harbour lights reflecting on the dark water. There was a new moon, sharp and bright. They raised their glasses to it.

'Bonne vacance!' said Noël.

'What?' said Mike.

The holiday had an easy rhythm. While Mike dressed, hummed and listened to Radio Mozart from Marseille, Noël would go down to the harbour and have a café crème at one of the many coffee bars and attempt to read a local paper. Then he would go to the covered market for bread, cheese, wine and fruit. There was a selection of prepared dishes of exceptionally good quality and he took a couple of portions back and put them in the fridge for their evening meal. Le Petit Chevrier had a good stock of books, which they worked their way through over the ten days. Lunch was usually in the courtyard at the back, sheltered by an ornate stone wall which was all that remained of a medieval monastery. As they ate their bread and cheese bright lizards would dart out of cracks in the wall to stare at them. Mike called them his dragons and they became quite tame as the days went by. After lunch with a glass of cold beer they both snoozed in the cool, stone-flagged interior, where there was a sofa for each of them. Late afternoon saw them arm in arm making their way slowly over the cobbles, between the cottage doorways flanked by hollyhocks. Mike found cobbles difficult, but as Noël said 'We can do anything we want, so long as we do it slowly.'

Down by the harbour there were ice-creams of all persuasions, and crisp waffles. Teatime was different every day.

They explored the island in the middle of the harbour where there were narrow alleys, intriguing shops and a lively art gallery. On some days they took a bus to another part of the island, passing acres of desolate salt pans. They lunched in shady village squares, but always missed their conversations with the lizards. Mike couldn't have been happier, and Noël gradually relaxed. It had been a bit of a gamble taking Mike so far from home, but it seemed to be working.

'How was France then?' bawled Blodwen. 'Must have been good. You're lookin' bloody years younger. Where next then? Or are you considerin' doin' a bit of work?'

'We'll see what ideas come up. I'd like Mike to choose next time.'

Jean hailed him and pointed to a pile of books and DVDs.

'These are all for you,' she said. 'Chief wants six reviews for next weekend. Then there's an assessment and evaluation session next Thursday.'

'What time?'

'Two-thirty. You'll need to bring your project overview, evaluation questionnaire and progress report.'

Noël groaned deeply.

18. Eco-Pages

'Anchovies,' said Noël. 'Poor little devils.'

'What?'

'We had anchovies last Christmas. You asked me whether they had feelings.'

'And?'

'Of course they do! There's a book I'm reviewing for the paper, and it talks about acknowledging the pain we feel for other species. It's true, when you asked me that question I did feel a stab of guilt – you could call it pain.'

'No more anchovies then I suppose.'

'Well I'd certainly think twice about it.' Noël was reading 'Active Hope' by Joanna Macy, which was deep ecology and turning much of his world inside out. 'I don't think the people of Yorkshire are ready for this book yet, but if they ignore all it says we're in for trouble. We're in for trouble anyway of course.'

'What sort of trouble?'

'Using up natural resources trouble. Filling the atmosphere with CO_2 trouble. Too many people on the planet trouble.'

'Has this woman got the answer then?' asked Mike.

'Not one answer of course, but she recommends that we try to slow things down while we change our way of thinking. She calls this time we're living in "The Great Turning".'

'Bit late for us old blokes though,' said Mike. 'Not much we can do.'

'I think Eddie would disagree with you,' said Noël. 'He's very much up with this sort of thinking. That's why they try to live lightly. I must lend him this book and get his ideas on it.' Noël put the book on one side and heaved up another.

'This is a monster volume,' he said. 'Lots of pictures though, so it shouldn't take too long.' This was 'Meme Wars,' a book aimed at economics students, encouraging them to challenge financial systems which take little account of the real world and real people. The Chief, or maybe Jean, was certainly feeding him with some interesting stuff.

'We're going to go Big,' said the Chief at the start of the next meeting. 'Going from a page to a full supplement.'

Peter sighed.

49

'Well at least I've found one really good story this week,' he said. 'People are moving their money from the big banks and putting it into ethical banks. There's an ethical bank in Bristol that has doubled in size over the last year.'

'I know the one,' said Noël. I moved my microscopic savings into it a couple of years ago. Nice people on the phone, and you can find out exactly what they are doing with your money. It's all in the public domain.'

'I'm planning to go down and interview the manager,' said Peter. And if the funds will run to it I'd like to do some more research down there. Bristol seems to be leading the way in this Eco-sort of thing.'

'Do something for the kids page then too,' roared Blodwen. 'See if they do children's accounts where rich grannies can put cash away for them.'

'Do rich grannies still exist?' wondered Noël.

'Well all the bloody money must be somewhere!' said Blodwen. 'It can't have fallen off the edge of the planet.'

'Most of it doesn't exist,' said Peter wearily. 'It's just created by private banks as debt, and then recorded as numbers on computers. No jingling bags of gold any more.'

'That's right,' said Noël. 'The great hefty book I've just been reviewing says a lot about that. Money's become a fiction, a story that we all pretend to believe in.'

'What if we all stopped pretending then?' shouted Blodwen as she left the room. There was a thoughtful silence. Noël felt in his pocket and took out a handful of coins. 'Just going round the corner for a sandwich,' he said. 'I wonder what would happen if they refused to accept coins for food.'

'Or what if they just gave it to you,' said Peter. I've been looking into The Gift Economy. The people of Ladakh in Northern India seem to be able to manage that way. Or they did until Western culture got its hooks into them.'

'There's a DVD on Ladakh waiting here for you Noël,' said Jean.

'Yes, that's the one I nicked the other night to watch,' said Peter. 'You'll find that all the social change that has happened to us over the last 200 years happened in about 15 years in Ladakh. There are still people alive there who remember how it used to be. Their reactions to Western culture are pretty revealing.'

Noël pondered on the fact that Peter, for all his sighing cynicism, seemed to be considering ideas that he would have scorned not many months ago.

'A couple of women from Ladakh were brought to London by the film-maker, to see where our culture had taken us,' went on Peter. 'What shocked them more than anything was our old folks' homes. They wept when they saw old people alone in single rooms staring at the telly.'

Noël nodded grimly. Those armchairs.

'Their old people were part of the family right to the end,' said Peter. 'They helped look after the little ones, and the little ones teased them and loved them….' his voice trailed off.

'What's up Peter?' said Noël. He'd never before seen emotion cross his colleague's face.

'My father,' said Peter. 'He ended up in a psychiatric hospital with Alzheimer's. We couldn't cope with him at home. I'll never forget the day we took him in – he had a lucid moment and said "How could you bring me to a place like this?"'

'Come and talk to me and Mike sometime,' said Noël. 'We've got quite a lot of experience between us.'

'Thanks.' Peter left the room abruptly.

19. The Fall

'The trouble with Mike is that most of the time he's perfectly normal.'

'And that's a trouble?' said Eddie, sliding a mug of tea across to Noël.

Margot advanced shyly and tried to climb on Noël's knee. He picked her up and gave her a hug. She looked up at him.

'Nice hair!' she said and ran her fingers through it.

'Long time since a girl did that,' smiled Noël. 'Things are looking up!'

'What's this trouble with normal then?' said Eddie again.

'Well, we're just being a couple of blokes, getting on with things. Then suddenly he'll say or do something completely off-beam. Totally illogical. Because I'm not expecting it I sometimes react impatiently, as I would with anyone else who hadn't had a stroke. Then he's upset of course and gets terribly anxious.'

'Tricky,' said Eddie. 'You can't be on the alert all the time. You'd be knackered.'

'I do get knackered, as you so sweetly put it. Then of course I'm even less patient. Mike's very quick to forgive if I've snapped at him – one of the benefits of short-term memory loss. I think I feel worse than he does.'

'Well perhaps it's one of those things you have to accept as part of the journey,' said Eddie. 'Take it in your stride. Don't beat yourself up about it. Say to Mike, and yourself, "I'm a hasty bugger. Sorry." Then it's all over.'

'I'll give it a try,' said Noël.

'Right. More tea?'

'No thanks. I must get back to the old devil. Looking after him seems to be teaching me a lot about myself. I thought I knew me!'

'That's how it goes,' said Eddie. 'Margot has the same effect on us.'

When Noël got home and opened the front door his heart stopped. Mike was lying on the floor at the foot of the stairs. His trousers were half down and there was blood on the floor by his head.

'Christ! Mike! What's happened?' shouted Noël, rushing over and crouching down. Flashbacks to the story told by the

Peacehaven security guard seared his brain. He put out a hand to touch him, but Mike moved his head slightly and Noël held back.

'Hi Noley,' he said in a muffled voice. 'Knew you'd be back soon so I waited here.'

Relief swept through Noël's body as he reached for his mobile and rang 999.

'Don't move him. We'll be there in minutes.'

Noël found a thick travel rug in a chest in the hall and laid it carefully over Mike.

'Help's coming soon old man.'

The paramedics were cheerful and efficient while checking him over.

'Nothing broken, but we need to take you into hospital to be sure there's nothing we've missed.'

They eased him on to a stretcher and Noël followed them into the ambulance.

'What happened Mike? Can you remember?'

'I'd run out of poo-roll in the *en-suite*,' said Mike plaintively. The paramedic looked slightly bemused.

'Go on Mike. I'll translate later,' said Noël.

'Thought I'd get some from the cloakroom. Came out of my room. Turned right. Smash.'

'Your trousers must have slipped and tripped you up.'

'Ah.' Mike hummed a little.

'Got it,' grinned the paramedic. 'Can I take some personal details now?'

'I can fill those in if you like,' said Noël.

'It's OK. We like to ask the patient if possible. It's a good way to check on brain function after a fall.'

Mike had a couple of stitches in the cut on his temple and was to be kept in overnight for observation. Noël took a taxi home. He was too shaken to mess about with buses.

The house was very still. No humming. No music. No tap of Mike's walking stick. No cheerful 'Hey Noley, what's for supper?'

I know Mike's OK. I should be feeling glad and free. Free of all responsibility for a while. Just me to cook for. I can read uninterrupted all evening. But here I am feeling that a chunk has been taken out of me. A pound of flesh out of my side –

more like a couple of kilos. Noël slept poorly and kept waking up to listen.

The next morning he rang Beth and Eddie. Beth was full of concern, more for Noël than Mike. She knew Noël would be feeling that he could have prevented the accident.

'You're a wonderful friend to Mike,' she said. 'Without you he'd have died of boredom in that awful place.'

'But…'

'You can't be with him every minute of the day. He'd hate it. Imagine yourself with someone at your elbow all the time.'

'True, but…'

'Old people sometimes fall over. So do most people. It's a fact of life. You just have to deal with it when it happens – which you did.'

'Umm…'

'Let's just be happy that he's OK.'

'OK. I'll try not to fuss. I'm fetching him home this afternoon if the doctors give him the all-clear.'

'Great. Give him our love.'

Noël gave the faint blood-stain on the parquet floor another scrub. He noticed with a start that Mike's head must have missed the cast-iron umbrella-stand by about two inches. He went cold. Out came the umbrellas and sticks and the hideous thing went out into the garage. He'd never liked it anyway.

20. Beth's surprise

It was Friday and the sun was shining. After about a fortnight of rain it was a relief. Noël was singing to himself in the kitchen as he washed up the breakfast things.

'Where are we going today?' asked Mike as he tapped in and sat down on the big chair by the window. Noël sighed. He had already explained several times that morning.

'I told you already,' he said testily. 'We're going into town to the Post Office, and then we're going to have lunch on the boat with Beth and Eddie. I want to lend Eddie a couple of these books to get some feedback.'

'What books are we going to buy?' said Mike.

Noël breathed deeply before answering. Mike was finding it increasingly difficult to follow a sequence of information. His short term memory had got much worse since his fall.

'We'll see what they've got,' said Noël in the end. It didn't really matter that they weren't going to a bookshop. By the time they got into town Mike would have forgotten what they were going for anyway. Noël hated himself for thinking in this way. Mike deserved respect and proper answers even though his memory was rubbish.

'We're going to the Post Office first,' he added, his voice measured and careful. That at least was perfectly true. These mental gymnastics were wearing him down.

'Sorry I keep forgetting things Noley,' said Mike, quietly. 'It must get on your nerves.' Noël's heart felt a pang.

'Not a problem, old fruit!' he said cheerily. But it was.

Beth was taking up a great deal of the space in Archimedes. They had moved the table out and somehow managed to fit stools and a chair around. Margot snuggled up close to her mother on the bench-seat. She put her small hand on Beth's bump.

'Twins,' she said proudly.

'Oh Margot!' said Beth, laughing. 'We were saving that bit of news for later - for a special announcement with a glass of wine!'

'Is it true?' asked Noël. 'Are you really expecting twins?'

''Fraid so,' said Beth. 'And here we are grumbling about the world population.'

'Well they will be very special people, if they're anything like their parents,' said Noël.

'That's the lot though,' said Eddie. 'I'm having the chop!'

Mike looked horrified. 'What's the chop?' he said anxiously.

'Oh that's just a silly word for it,' said Eddie laughing. 'I'm having a vasectomy so that I can't give Beth any more babies.' Margot nodded wisely. Mike looked thoughtful. People of his generation had never considered such a thing.

'Pity though,' he said. 'I like babies.'

'The world has more than enough of them though, Mike,' said Eddie. 'The population will be nine billion by the middle of the century.'

'Can't think numbers that big,' said Mike. 'Head's too small.'

'You'll never manage on the boat with three children will you?' asked Noël.

'That's the other thing we wanted to talk to you about,' said Eddie. 'We could manage for a bit, while they are tiny, but we're going to have to think seriously about moving.'

'Any ideas where you might go?' asked Noël.

'I want somewhere with a bit of land,' said Eddie. 'The allotment's OK but I'd like to grow more, keep some chickens, even a small house cow. The trouble is we don't have the money to buy that sort of place – we'd have to rent.'

'You probably wouldn't want to put endless work into land that wasn't yours,' observed Noël.

'Oh that's not the problem,' said Eddie. 'The land is the land, and I'd like to make somewhere flourish and fruitful. I don't have to possess it. You can't possess land anyway – we're only tenants in this world.'

Noël instinctively pulled himself up. Yes I know that very well, he thought. I was just talking like an idiot. Nobody would think you'd understood a word of what you've been reading for the Eco-Pages, he scolded himself. We've lived too long thinking we're lords of creation. If, after reading all that earth wisdom you catch yourself thinking like an unreformed materialist what hope is there for the readers of your articles? He shook his head briskly, trying to get rid of the old unwanted concepts which clung like torn cobwebs in the corners of his mind.

'We don't have much money,' Eddie went on. 'We just pay our way with the part-time wood-working that I do. I'd like to keep it that way if possible. Perhaps join a community somewhere.'

'We'd hate to lose you,' said Noël. Mike looked anxious.

'Have they got lost?' he asked. 'Don't they know where they are?'

'They are looking for a new place to live,' explained Noël. 'When the twins come along it's going to get a bit crowded on Archimedes.'

'They can live with us,' said Mike. 'No problem.'

Everybody laughed. 'Good old Mike,' said Eddie. 'I knew you'd have the answer.'

Noël however did not laugh. He stared at Mike in astonishment as an idea began, very slowly, to form in his mind. Now don't be hasty, he said to himself. Go home and think about it properly. He raised his glass and smiled.

'Here's to the future.'

After Mike had gone to bed that night Noël sat at the kitchen table with a glass of whisky and pencil and paper. How many rooms do Mike and I really need? How many spare? Kitchens? Bathrooms? Independent access? The idea of having Beth and Eddie and their children bringing the house to life kept him awake until the small hours. There were two acres of land around Treetops; Eddie could almost farm it. Some of the trees would have to go, but not many. Noël had no children to leave the property to, and he knew his sister wouldn't want it. It was his to do as he liked with. It was four o'clock when he eventually climbed the stairs, and he dozed restlessly until the sun came up.

'That was a great idea of yours Mike,' said Noël over the morning coffee.

'What idea was that?'

'About having Beth and Eddie to live with us here.'

'Oh good. When are they coming?'

'I haven't invited them yet,' laughed Noël. 'They might well have other ideas.'

'I hope not,' said Mike. 'They're nice.'

'Let's go down and see them again,' continued Noël. 'I've got a DVD to watch and write about this morning. Then we'll go and ask them. I'll give them a ring and see if they're in.'

'Hope they won't have gone away by then,' said Mike.

'No it's OK. They've got to have the twins first!' said Noël. Secretly he was extremely anxious that Eddie might contact some new-age commune in the Dales. They were so young and lively. Would they really want to come and live with a couple of old blokes in a Victorian mansion surrounded by dark pine trees? Mike was getting more difficult to deal with, and Noël himself was beginning to feel his age. He wouldn't be much good at working the land when he finally retired from *The Voice of the North* at the end of next year. He would be the one in the armchair before too long.

It was significant that the DVD Noël was reviewing that morning was the one about Ladakh that Peter had mentioned. The images that struck Noël most forcibly were of the old people of the Ladakh community. One toothless grandad sat on the steps of his house with a little child on his knee, and they were both grinning with delight. In another scene the family were sitting round sharing a meal. A toddler took a handful of corn, crept up behind an old man and trickled it playfully on his bald head. The joyfulness of their shared life radiated from their faces. There was so much singing and laughter that the film-maker felt it necessary to explain in the commentary that they were not putting on a show for the camera. She had lived alongside them for many years and this is genuinely how it was. It was harrowing to see how this was later affected with the coming of tourism, imported foods and Western Culture.

When he'd finished his review and send it in Noël sat for a while thinking how to put it to Beth and Eddie. What, in effect, he wanted to do was to give them a share in his home on the understanding that after his day it would become their own. That's a pretty big gift, and in these days when money rules the world gifts are often regarded with suspicion. He remembered the first time there was a Give or Take Day in the town. The local Transition group had taken a church hall and invited people to bring unwanted items. Then on the day the public had been invited in to take anything that they wanted. People were both delighted and slightly uncomfortable.

'Don't we have to pay?' several of them had asked. 'Donations or something?'

'No. It's all absolutely free. No money needed today at all. It will help keep stuff out of landfill.' The Transition volunteers had laughed a lot when they saw a young man with some garden tools under his arm creep out of the door and then run furtively down the road as if he was a criminal. It had also made them laugh when the caretaker of the hall had given them a stern warning beforehand.

'You realise that while that stuff is in here it won't be insured?'

'Why would we want to insure it?' they had asked.

'Well somebody might take something,' said the caretaker.

'Er… that's what it's all about!'

Excluding money from human transactions has almost become extinct, thought Noël. We pay people to look after our old people, and then grumble when they don't do it properly. One of the books he had read recently said 'every time you pay someone you are getting them to do something you could probably do yourself.'

'Come on Mike,' called Noël. 'Get your skates on. We'll go down and see what they think of your brilliant idea.'

'What idea's that?' asked Mike. 'Who are we going to see?'

'We're going to lunch with Beth and Eddie on the boat again,' said Noël patiently, 'and we're going to invite them to come and live with us.' Remembering again Cecil's way of coping with repeated questions was very helpful. This was the fourth time Noël had answered this one this morning, and every time his answer had been a little different, but always good-humoured. Good old Cecil.

'Oh what a good idea!' said Mike happily. 'You always have good ideas Noley.'

21. A shock

Two shots rang out, then after a short pause a third. There was a scream and Margot ran into the saloon with blood running down the side of her face. Beth ran through from the galley and scooped her up.

'What? What happened?'

There were sounds of a scuffle out on the towpath and Beth heard Eddie shouting louder than she had ever heard him shout. Margot was clutching her tight and there was blood on Beth's shoulder. Still hugging Margot, Beth went out on deck. Eddie had a young lad in an arm-lock and was bellowing in his ear.

It was Saturday and the gang had a plan that morning. They were all fired up, but Craig didn't want to take part. He'd tried to suggest a different plan, but they rounded on him and called him a sissy. They had circled him chanting 'Craig's a wimp, Craig's a girly.' He had stormed off and left them to it. If that meant more bullying at school, well, he was getting used to it. He'd joined the gang for protection, but he hated them.

Craig stormed along under the trees along the towpath, digging his heels into the soft gravel. Whenever he saw a larger stone he would kick it fiercely into the water. He hated them. He would never have anything more to do with them. They had been 'magging' girls on the way home from school, which was bad enough, but fairly harmless. It only frightened them. Yesterday though one of the bolder girls had stood up to them and laughed in their faces. When they had cornered her in an alleyway and then stood round in a circle and one by one exposed themselves she had just laughed. Then she just pushed them aside and walked away.

'I'll tell my friends which was the smallest!' she'd called back over her shoulder, and then run off round the corner. The boys were stunned, then furious.

'We'll show her,' shouted Spanner, the leader. 'We'll get her - and then do it. All of us.' This was bold talk. Although they all bragged, their sexual experience amounted to very little in total. Craig knew, however, that things could turn very nasty indeed and he wanted no part of it.

As Craig rounded the bend past the lock gates he saw a narrow-boat moored by the tow-path. On the roof were troughs with plants and on the deck was a semi-circle of small pots with cuttings in. The semi-circle reminded him of the gang and he picked up a stone and hurled it at the larger of the pots. 'That's you, Spanner,' he thought as the pot fell over and earth scattered across the deck. He found more stones and hurled them wildly. One hit the roof with a crack. Then another. Then just as he hurled the third a little girl looked out of the cabin door. The stone ricocheted off the corner of the cabin and struck her in the face. She screamed and tumbled back inside.

'What the hell do you think you're doing?' Eddie, who had just arrived back from town, threw down his bike and grabbed Craig from behind, fixing him firmly in an arm-lock. He pushed him to the ground and knelt on his chest, shouting in his face. Craig was terrified.

'Sorry. Didn't mean it. I was angry,' he gasped. Eddie pulled him to his feet and marched him on to the boat and into the cabin. Beth was bathing Margot's face. The stone had struck her on the right temple, perilously close to her eye. Beth was sobbing, Margot was trembling and clinging to her.

'Say you're sorry, you creep,' shouted Eddie. Craig managed a strangled 'sorry' but he was near to tears himself. Margot began to cry again. She had never heard her father shout before, and it frightened her.

'Don't move,' said Eddie to Craig, and rammed him in a corner. Eddie went to the galley and brought a glass of water for Beth. 'It's OK,' he said, calmer now. 'It's only a small cut – and it missed her eye thank God.'

Beth shuddered and took the glass with shaking hands. Margot loosed her hold on her mother and pulled a cushion towards her. She curled up with it and seemed to go to sleep.

'Children are amazing!' said Eddie. 'Look at that. She's lucky that she can't imagine all the things that might have happened. But you - you're quite old enough to realise what you were doing was stupid and dangerous. You could see there were people living on this boat, couldn't you?'

'Didn't think,' said Craig. 'I was blind angry.'

'What about?' asked Eddie. Craig gave a muttered account of what had happened to him that morning, leaving out quite a few of the details. 'The gang turned on me,' he ended.

'OK,' Said Eddie. 'Will we go to your Mum and Dad now, or to the police?'

'Please not the police,' pleaded Craig. 'It would upset my Mum too much. Got no Dad,' he added. 'I'm truly sorry. I'll do anything…'

'I'll keep you to that,' said Eddie. 'Right. Let's go. I'll take you home.'

'Don't forget Noël and Mike are coming to lunch again,' said Beth. 'I was just making the soup. They've got some plan or other they want to talk about.'

'I'll be back as soon as I've sorted this idiot out,' said Eddie and frog-marched Craig off the boat.

'What's that plaster on your face, Margot?' asked Mike as he came aboard.

'Naughty boy,' said Margot.

Beth filled in the story as she laid the table, poured some beer and brought the bowls of soup.

'It wasn't what you'd call a crime,' said Eddie when he got back. 'Just total thoughtlessness. He was pretty shocked at what he'd done, particularly when he saw how he'd hit her so close to her eye. He was in quite a state when I left him at home. I told his mother about the bullying too, so maybe something positive will come of it. I'm going to keep him to his promise of doing something to make up for it though. It will do him more good than any number of police cautions.'

'It's silly,' said Beth, 'but it's made me really nervous about having children on the boat. It shouldn't do, as it was just a one-off thing, but it does.'

'Well it's funny you should say that,' said Noël. We've an idea to tell you about that might have turned up just at the right moment. It was Mike's idea actually.'

'Was it?' said Mike. 'Oh good! Let's hear it then Noley.'

Beth and Eddie listened carefully while Noël outlined the proposal. 'It could be a temporary solution while you get the twins established in your lives,' he said. 'We barely use the top floor and it would make a spacious flat. There would have to be some work done on it of course.'

'Well we could chip in with that,' said Eddie. 'I can do all the woodwork myself of course, and we'd have some money from selling Archimedes.'

'Wouldn't it drive you mad having three children bombing around the place?' asked Beth. 'You're both used to such a quiet life.'

'Too quiet,' said Mike. 'I love children. I could read to them. Edgar never liked being read to - he was always outside tearing around. I know Margot likes stories.'

Margot moved across to Mike and put her hands on his thin knees.

'Story now?' she asked, smiling winningly.

'Not just now Margot,' said her mother. 'We're still eating and talking. We're talking about going to live in Noël's house.'

'There's a garden!' cried Margot. 'We can have chickings!' She danced round the table clapping her hands above her head. 'Come on chicks! Here's your dinner!'

'We could certainly grow a lot of our own stuff up there,' said Eddie. 'A few trees would have to go, but the soil is good. I've had a poke around it and was thinking of asking you if we could garden a bit of it.'

'Let's not rush into anything we might regret,' said Noël. 'Take some time to think about it. List the pros and cons and we can talk again soon.'

'Don't leave it too long,' said Beth. 'The twins are getting restless!'

22. Partnerships

Jean looked up as Noël came into the newspaper office and shook out his umbrella. A young lad with a shock of ginger hair was sitting next to her.

'Meet Freddie, my new assistant.'

'Hi Freddie,' said Noël. 'Is Jean treating you well?'

Freddie nodded and looked down. He didn't seem to know how to respond. Jean answered for him. 'Freddie's a highly competent computer expert, just what we need. The future of *The Voice of the North* is to be totally interactive online, and he's going to help us with the finer points of setting it up.'

'Is that what today's meeting is about?' asked Noël.

'No, not today. The Chief has an idea for another column in the Eco-Pages and he wants our input.'

The Chief was rubbing his hands as they all sat down round the table. '"An idea whose time has come,"' he beamed, quoting Victor Hugo. 'The Eco-Pages have put up our weekend circulation by 20% this year so far, and we're going to add to it.'

His idea was for a small-ad section based on local environmental activities. 'Local can mean Yorkshire-wide, and it would be for partnerships between people and green activities.'

'Per'aps Noël can find himself a good woman at last then,' roared Blodwen. 'About time, before he turns into an old woman 'imself.'

'Now Blod,' said Noël. 'Just because I'm looking after someone and cooking a bit more it doesn't make me go female. Men can care too you know.'

'Get on!' shrieked Blodwen. 'Only raggin'.'

To start with they were going to give space to people with gardens or land that they couldn't manage, and try to pair them up with people looking for space to grow food. 'What a coincidence,' thought Noël. 'There must be many people in both those positions.'

'We can also take some personal ads,' said the Chief. 'No reason why people shouldn't find green partners that way as well. Green Partners could cover many projects and developments.'

Peter looked up. He had been doodling on his note-pad.

'Would you like us to draft a few sample ads to get things going?' he asked. Noël turned and stared at him in surprise. This wasn't the sceptical Peter of old.

They dispersed and Noël picked up the latest batch of books and DVDs to review. His hot-desk was vacant for the time being so he sat down with a cup of coffee. It was good to be back in the office atmosphere for a while.

'I actually miss all this,' he thought as Blodwen, in the middle distance, vibrated the air-waves. He sat looking dreamily out of the window. Then he pulled his notepad towards him and began to write:

Cellist wanted. Dark curly hair, soft eyes, exquisite hands, quirky sense of humour, slightly foreign accent. Partnership offered in warm household.

He looked at it for a while, then tore the page out and crushed it very gently. The image came back to him again of Ella Kolevich. She had been found dead, with her arms wrapped tightly around her cello case. A victim of *The Herald of Free Enterprise* ferry disaster in 1987. Ella had been on her way to Brussels to play in a concert with her quartet.

His world had been torn apart.

The way they had first met was like a short story in itself. In fact he had written it as such to try to ease the pain of his loss, but had never published it. He kept the typescript in the library drawer with the CDs. With her quartet's recording of the Brahms.

The Singer, not the Song

Noël Burke turned up his collar, hunched his shoulders and tried to slip across the foyer. As he sidled behind a chattering group near the exit a lady in a red velvet jacket turned and spotted him.

'Ah Noël!' she boomed, touching his shoulder in an archly possessive manner. 'And what will you be penning for your column tonight?'

'Erm – probably do it tomorrow,' he mumbled. Wrestling a smile he continued 'It takes a little time to get one's thoughts in order you know.'

'Well, we thought she was wonderful,' said the thin lady in black lace, 'and so tragic,' she added, raising her eyes to the ceiling.

'Er yes,' said Noël. Then hastily: 'Sorry must dash. Got to make a phone call.'

Once home he threw his coat down, dropped into an armchair and dialled a number speedily.

'Annie! Sorry to ring so late. D'you happen to know who Tatiana Kolevich's agent is?' He nodded as he jotted down an address. 'Oh Penny Hansford is it? I used to know her. I'll give her a ring tomorrow. Thanks Annie.'

The entrance to Hansford Artists glittered with steel and plate glass. As Noël pushed the door open the smell of new carpet tickled his nose and he sneezed. The girl with the sculpted bronze hair looked up from the reception desk.

'Can I help you?'

'Yes please. May I speak to Penny Hansford?'

'I'll see if she's free. Your name?'

'Burke. Noël Burke. She may remember me.'

'Noël how lovely to see you!' Penny Hansford proffered a scented cheek for a kiss. 'Come and sit down. What are you up to these days?'

'Oh this and that. Freelance journalism mostly. Some music articles. You know the sort of thing.'

'Splendid. So what brings you here?'

'I believe you're handling Tatiana Kolevich.'

'That's right. What a find! Such a pity she's only here for one week, but it's been full houses every night so far.'

'When does she go back to Russia?'

'On Sunday. She did a small arts centre over your way in Helmsley last night.'

'Yes I know. I was there.'

'And her final recital is here in Leeds Town Hall tonight. I hope you'll give her a brilliant write-up.'

Noël shifted uncomfortably and his eyes avoided Penny's expectant gaze. She turned to pick up a glossy brochure from her desk and continued enthusiastically.

'This is her publicity stuff. Good isn't it?'

Noël glanced at it briefly, then looked again more closely.

'When was this taken?' he asked.

'Just before she came I think,' said Penny. 'Do you want one? We've plenty left.'

'Yes – thanks.' Noël folded the leaflet and slipped it into an inside pocket. Then he rose and stretched out a hand. 'Sorry I must go. Got to do some research at the library.'

'But you haven't said why you came,' said Penny surprised.

'Oh – just hoped for a photo!' he said, avoiding her eyes and touching his breast pocket. 'Thanks for this.' He left awkwardly, sneezing once more as he crossed the entrance hall.

'Odd chap!' said Julie the receptionist, watching his flapping raincoat crossing the road. 'He didn't stay long.'

'Oh Noël's OK,' said Penny. 'I think he was a bit smitten with Tatiana.'

'Isn't everybody!' laughed Julie.

In the library Noël sat at a table with the largest Russian dictionary he could find. He pulled out his notebook and started cross-checking and making notes. Once he laughed out loud, muffling it quickly with his hand as he wrote. Then he went to Leeds Town Hall and checked the time of the evening concert. There was just time to get home for a shower and a bite to eat before the performance.

Tatiana Kolevich sat on the bed in her hotel room and looked at herself critically.

'Not bad,' she said and smiled a satisfied smile.

'What do you mean "not bad"' replied her reflection, or rather the almost identical girl seated beside her on the bed. 'I think I look brilliant!'

Tatiana stood up, took the other girl by the shoulders and steered her round behind the stool, then sat down again. Two animated faces smiled, one above the other, and two mops of dark curls began to quiver as they started laughing helplessly.

Noël put his empty glass on the bar and joined the shuffling crowd making its way back into the auditorium for the second half of the concert. As he sat down he frowned and scratched his temple with the top of his pencil. His programme, as usual, was covered with notes in his small, neat writing. Tatiana came on to the platform to a roar of applause and started to sing the first of a set of Russian folk-songs that she had sung the previous night in Helmsley. Suddenly Noël smiled, put away his notes, folded his arms and sat back.

There was quite a crowd backstage waiting for Tatiana after the performance. Noël held back waiting for them to disperse and then, just as she was about to reach for her coat he came forward, notebook in hand.

'I'm from the press. May I ask a few questions?'

'Of course. Come in and sit down.' She brushed a curl back from her forehead and sat down facing him. 'What would you like to know?'

'Well, first of all, where's Tatiana?' said Noël quietly.

The singer rose and went to close the dressing-room door. 'What do you mean?' she said, lightly, sitting down again. 'I am Tatiana.'

'It seemed to me,' said Noël, 'that the singer of the first half of the programme, and the singer of the folk-song sequence in the second half…..'

Tatiana leant forward, opened her mouth to speak and then started laughing.

'Oh well,' she said, 'there's no point in trying to cover up. It's too late now anyway. Tatiana, my sister – my twin sister – has gone off with her English lover. I shall take her place right up to the point of departure tomorrow to give her a good start. Then I shall disappear at the airport, change clothes and leave by another exit. I can see you are not the sort of person to spoil our plan with publicity.'

Noël had pocketed his notebook and was smiling.

'But tell me,' she continued, 'how could you tell? Nobody else did.'

'You were a bit naughty with the folk-songs,' said Noël. 'You did the Helmsley concert too didn't you?'

'Yes. That was a sort of rehearsal for tonight. I changed the words about a bit for my own amusement. All those old ladies there – how would they know the difference?'

'And that tiny mole on your chin, which reminds me of my sister's,' said Noël, leaning forward and wiping it off with the corner of his handkerchief. 'I noticed it in Tatiana's photograph, but it wasn't there at Helmsley.'

'No. I forgot. What a fool I am!'

'What's *your* name then?' asked Noël. 'Are you a professional singer too?'

'I'm Ella, and I'm a 'cellist but we both studied singing when we were young. I play with the Arriaga Quartet. Here's our publicity card.'

'Can I take you anywhere?' asked Noël, pocketing the card carefully and getting up to leave.

'No, thank you. The hotel has arranged a taxi for Tatiana, and I must keep up my act.'

'Then perhaps you'd better replace the mole,' said Noël. Then, slightly ruefully, 'I hope Tatiana will be happy with her man.'

He left by the stage door, walked purposefully to the corner, then he stopped. He took out his handkerchief and held it to his nose. A faint perfume lingered on it. He touched it to his lips, sighed, and set off for home.

23. Reconstructions

It was through the Green Pages that Noël had found the architect. Craine and Forsyth specialised in sympathetic conversions of old buildings using authentic materials. It wasn't that Treetops was particularly beautiful. It had that self-conscious grandeur so beloved of Victorian industrialists, but Noël wanted it to keep as much of its integrity as possible. 'No carbuncles on the face of our house,' he joked with Mike.

'Carbuncles? They can be awfully painful,' said Mike. 'My father had them.'

Beth's twins had arrived a couple of weeks early, possibly due to the shock of Craig's stone-throwing episode. They were two healthy little boys. Margot was beside herself with delight. 'I can help Mummy when she's tired,' she bubbled on the phone when the news came through. 'They are tiny, tiny.'

Eddie was working on ideas for the library at Treetops, to put to the architect. Noël wanted to make it into a living space for himself. He'd always hated the rather bleak bedroom upstairs where he usually slept.

'You could have a bed that folds up and disappears into the bookcases,' said Eddie. 'I could make that, and then a cupboard that had a miniature kitchen in it. Just a little sink, hob and a couple of small wall cupboards. Like on the boat.

'I'm going to be using the main kitchen,' said Noël. 'I wouldn't really need that.

'You have to think of possible future uses,' said Eddie. 'Easier to do the plumbing now than later. Maybe the architects could fit an en-suite in, back-to-back with Mike's. When is he coming up to take a look?'

'Next Thursday,' said Noël. 'There's a Hilary Forsyth coming who is presumably one of the partners. Apparently he specialises in Victorian buildings.'

Noël had been to collect cardboard boxes from the supermarket. They were piled in the library and he was packing up all his father's old science books. They were to go to the University bookshop where they could be sold on second-hand to the students. Any that were totally out of date could be passed on to a charity shop. This left a large section of the bookcases free for Eddie's conversion ideas.

The following Wednesday, as Noël was drinking a mug of coffee, he saw the figure of a young man pass the kitchen window. He seemed to be looking at the house very carefully, hands in pockets as he walked.

'Cheek!' thought Noël. 'What does he think he's doing?' He put down his mug and went to the back door. 'Hey! What are you doing?'

The figure turned and smiled. Noël suddenly realised that it was a young woman in jeans and Doc Martens with a man's cap on her head.

'Sorry to give you a fright,' she said as she came towards him with an outstretched hand. 'My name's Hilary. Hilary Forsyth. I'm meant to be coming to see you tomorrow but I happened to be passing and thought I'd take a preliminary look. It was a bit cheeky.'

'That's fine by me,' said Noël, rather delighted by her wide smile and open manner. 'Would you like to come in for a coffee?'

'I'll just complete the circuit, then yes, I'd love that.'

Noël went back inside and put the kettle on. At that moment Mike came tapping in, so Noël got out two more mugs.

'I'll come up tomorrow as arranged with all my gear,' said Hilary as she leant back with legs crossed, hugging her coffee mug. 'Just give me a clue as to what you want to do.'

'We want to split the house into two. Upstairs for a family and downstairs for us two.'

'Do you want to be completely separate, with independent access?'

'Well not really, but for the future that might become necessary I suppose.'

'We can probably make it possible both ways. It's something we often do.'

'Thinking ahead for both of us, I also wondered about installing a small lift,' said Noël. 'That would make the whole building usable for young and old. Do such things exist?'

'Oh yes, there are plenty of choices these days. Some take minimal space and disturbance to install.'

Noël went on to explain about Eddie's woodworking talent, and his ideas for the library. Hilary liked the sound of it and looked forward to meeting him. They parted in high spirits, looking forward to making something exciting out of the staid old house.

'Great girl that!' said Mike. 'She looks like a boy. Lovely smile.'

'Yes. Lovely smile.'

Noël got Google Maps up on the screen, and then searched on 'Yorkshire care homes'. An unpleasant rash of pink spots spread across the screen. What was the name that Cecil and Emily had mentioned? Was it in Scarborough or Whitby? There were too many to check out, so he rang Emily.

'While Treetops is being taken apart I would like to find somewhere good for Mike to stay,' he began. 'You told me about a Quaker retirement home some time ago, either in Scarborough or Whitby. Do you remember?'

'That would be Robin Hill Lodge in Whitby,' said Emily. 'It's a very happy place. Would you like me to contact them and see if they have a space for him?'

'That would be wonderful. The builders are planning to come during the last week in November. The worst should be over before Christmas.'

'I'll see what I can do.'

The very thought of any care home, Quaker or otherwise, made Noël feel queasy, but Beth and Eddie had been adamant.

'You're exhausted. You're looking pale and sick. You need a complete rest.' Beth went on to talk to him seriously about caring for Mike. 'You have to live your life too. When you get back we'll get down to organising some regular times when you can do your own thing. There's always help around if only you ask. So often it's pride that stops people asking.'

'That's very true,' said Noël. 'But I know Mike so well now. I can anticipate what he needs. A stranger couldn't do that.'

'But Mike needs to be able to function with others as well as you,' said Beth. 'To assume that you're the only person in the world who can look after him is….'

'Pride?' asked Noël.

'It could even be dangerous. What if something happens to you? Where would that leave him? He needs to practise coping with different people and unexpected happenings. That's real life.'

Noël could see the sense of this. He searched a holiday cottage website and found The Stationmaster's Office at

Holtby Monkton. It was tiny, so not too expensive, and was in a quiet village. He booked it for a week at the end of November.

'I'm coming back after a week,' he insisted. 'I'm looking forward to seeing how Hilary gets this whole thing together.'

24. A Week Alone

Noël rubbed the tender spot on his head.

'That spiral staircase is a menace,' he thought. 'I'll just do one review before I start my list.' He took a book off the pile. 'Active Hope' he wrote at the top of the page. Subtitle 'How to Face the Mess we're in without Going Crazy.'

'A good book to be reviewing today,' he said aloud. 'There are bigger problems than mine to worry about.'

His hand rose again to touch the sore spot. Then his eyelids began to droop. He moved over to the sofa and lay back on the cushions. Gradually he slipped sideways, tucked his long legs up beside him and hitched himself into a comfortable position. There was a thick rug draped over the back of the sofa and he pulled it round his shoulders.

The sky was completely dark when he woke. He looked at his watch and realised that he had slept for four hours. He still felt tired, so after some soup he climbed the spiral staircase and crawled into the bed under the eaves.

The next day he sat down to work again, but after half an hour he was back on the sofa. It wasn't until the third day that he managed to write the review. It was short and poignant. The main message of the book was that mankind should first be grateful for this wonderful planet and all that is on it. Secondly to acknowledge the pain that we feel when we think about what human exploitation is doing to it. Thirdly, to take steps to slow down the process of destruction. And finally to change completely anthropocentric ways of thinking, which caused most of the problems in the first place.

He tore out the sheet of paper, folded it up and slipped it into his brief-case. On the next page he drew two columns: Problems and Solutions. At the top he wrote an instruction to himself:

Whatever the problem is there is sure to be an intelligent solution. If you can't think of one yourself then ask your friends. You have some wise and wonderful friends, who will like to be asked. Don't be too proud to seek their advice. Most of the answers are already somewhere in your head.

He then began to list some of the problems connected with looking after Mike. Noël was now, in effect, what social services jargon termed 'a full-time carer'. As such, at Kay and Jim's suggestion, he and Mike had been formally 'assessed'. A young woman had called on them, inspected the house, and the new plans, and ticked a lot of boxes. Noël strongly disliked this invasion of his life. It classified him, and Mike, in a way that he found totally unacceptable. They were old friends. The terminology turned his life into a formula, a commodity, and separated him and Mike according to their different 'needs'. There was no doubt a monetary scale on which these needs were priced. He felt dehumanised. This separation of people from reality was the subject of the next book on his pile, 'The Rise of Humanity' and he was looking forward to reading it, but The List must be tackled first to clear the mess in his head.

The first item he wrote on the left-hand side was 'time to think'. At home although he was able to read and work in the kitchen or the library he was always on the alert. The slightest sound could not be ignored just in case it was Mike in some difficulty. Mike, usually so calm and easy-going, was getting increasingly impatient with himself when things went wrong, and the things that upset him were becoming increasingly trivial.

'Oh damn!' would come a shout, and the sound of Mike's chair scraping on the wooden floor. Noël would have to go through to see what had happened.

'What's up?'

'I just can't find the bookmark. It was here when I started reading and now it's gone. I'm just so stupid these days.'

'Don't upset yourself. Let's take a look round. Ah I've spotted it! You tucked it into the top of your cardigan – how very sensible!' Noël breathed deeply, trying not to let the triviality of the crisis wind him up.

'It's not sensible if I can't find it,' answered Mike crossly, but perfectly logically. Then 'thanks for finding it Noley. You're a pal.' Mike would smile and the whole episode would be forgotten, but Noël's concentration would be wrecked and sometimes a useful train of thought completely lost.

Solution? The right-hand column was invitingly blank, but so was his head. He put his pen down and went to put the kettle on. Then he sat in the stationmaster's armchair with a cup of tea, away from the table, and let his body relax. This time sleep didn't sweep over him, but he gradually began to think more clearly.

'If this was somebody else's problem what would I advise?' he asked himself. 'It's always so easy to give advice to others!'

'The answer, my friend, is not to try to do your work and look after Mike at the same time,' came the reply. 'It's setting you up for disaster before you've even begun. It gets your nerves and teeth on edge in the background of your mind, to coin a bizarre analogy. You won't do good work, and you won't be all that understanding when you have to go and help Mike.'

'What's the answer then?' asked Noël, rather startled that another part of his brain was talking so sensibly to him.

'How much time do you need for concentrated work each week?'

'I could probably do with three mornings a week – about three hours each morning.'

'Right. For three mornings a week you need to be away from the house to work.'

'But I can't leave Mike alone for all that time.'

'When Beth and Eddie move in he won't be alone.'

'But they'll have three children to look after, and they are entitled to their own lives.'

'Haven't you heard of 'Carer's Support'?'

Noël sulked. During the assessment the social worker had mentioned Carer's Support, but he had dismissed it as more jargon. He was a perfectly fit bloke and didn't need 'support' for heaven's sake. It was Mike that needed looking after.

'That's what Carer's Support does,' went on the voice in his head. 'They make it possible for carers to lead their own lives for a bit. I bet they could find someone to come in at least once a week and be available for Mike. They might even take him into town for a coffee, or for a ride up the Dales.'

'Well that would be good,' thought Noël. 'That's more than I feel like doing for him after a morning of interrupted work.'

'Exactly,' said the voice, smugly. 'Why have you got that grin on your face?'

'Well that's one morning taken care of,' said Noël petulantly. 'What about the others?'

'I'm perfectly sure that among your friends there are several who would enjoy talking to Mike and taking him out if you weren't so neurotically protective of him.'

'Now that's a bit nasty,' replied Noël, hurt.

76

'Think about it!' said the voice.

'Well Cecil might enjoy talking music with him sometimes…' mused Noël. 'He'd love to hear some of Mike's tales of the goings-on backstage at the Hallé. He'd never believe some of them!'

'There you are! That's two people's lives you've cheered up, and we've only just begun.'

'Ha!' said Noël aloud in a very Blodwen manner. He jumped up from the armchair and returned to the note-pad.

Strangely, in the silence of the little Stationmaster's Office, Noël's brain operated clearly and in a way that he had never before experienced. He covered sheets of paper with new ideas. He wrote some of the best reviews that he'd ever done. Best of all at the end of the week he was excited about getting back to Treetops and life with Mike.

'I never knew I had two people in my head!' he told Beth and Eddie when he got back. Beth smiled wisely, turned to Eddie and they nodded to each other.

'We've got all sorts of useful stuff in our heads,' said Eddie. 'We just don't sit in silence for long enough to listen to it. There's always some external racket going on. Sometimes we hide from ourselves inside noise.' They were walking across the market place together and a young lad passed them with his ears wired up to his pocket. 'Like that,' laughed Eddie.

Treetops was still a terrible mess, so Kay and Jim invited Noël to stay with them. At first he had resisted.

'It's OK. I can camp out in the kitchen on an air-bed,' he said. 'The builders won't be much longer.'

'Think how much nicer it would be to go up to the house refreshed every morning,' said Kay. 'Our spare room is empty. You can be a free agent and use it for as much of the day as you like. If you'd like a meal with us in the evening just let me know in the morning.'

Noël was becoming more aware of his personal pride and independence, getting in the way of a good solution. He smiled gratefully.

'Actually that would be wonderful,' he said. 'Thank you.'

'That's more like it,' said the voice in his head. 'You stuck-up bugger!'

Noël went over to Whitby to see how Mike was doing. He found him in the lounge which had enormous windows overlooking the harbour.

'It's great here,' said Mike. 'Just look at that! I see fishing boats and little ships coming and going all day. Better than the telly!'

The atmosphere at Robin Hill Lodge was warm, calm and friendly. Noël, who had been dreading the visit, began to relax. He sat in an armchair beside Mike, and only a small shiver ran up his spine.

'Would you like some coffee?' asked a gentle voice, and a tall grey-haired lady stood beside them.

'I was thinking of taking Mike out for coffee actually,' said Noël quickly.

'It's so cold out,' she replied. 'Wouldn't you be more comfortable here?'

'I'm watching you,' said Noël's inner voice.

'Yes, you're right,' said Noël. 'It's absolutely bitter today. The wind was blowing the car all over the place on the way over the tops. Let's have coffee here and watch the ships.'

They had a very happy couple of hours together. Noël told Mike about all the developments at the house, and a little bit about new plans for their future life together.

'When we're settled back in the house I'm hoping to invite more people in to see us,' said Noël. 'Hilary is planning something rather special for the front hall. Do you remember how dark and gloomy it was?'

'Like coming into a… into a… into a solicitor's office,' said Mike. 'All dark mahogany and gloomy corners.'

'Well it's going to be much lighter. She's found some huge Victorian windows from a demolition company, and she's putting them each side of the front door. They've got a bit of stained glass round the edges, but they're mainly clear. Then there's to be a wood-burning stove and a couple of sofas.'

'Good grief,' said Mike. It will be like another room.'

'The idea is to make it a meeting-place,' said Noël. 'Upstairs and downstairs can meet there for coffee in the mornings, if they want to. The children can bomb around.'

'What about the hot stove?' said Mike. Noël was touched by his clear thinking and his concern for the children.

78

'It will have a protective rail around it,' said Noël. 'Hilary thought of that. Actually she was thinking about the dog.'

'What dog?'

'Oh, she suggested we had a dog as another companion for you, and for the children upstairs. She said it's a dog sort of house!'

'It's going to be fun,' said Mike.

'Yes, it's going to be fun,' said Noël.

25. A place to work

All the heavy building work was done by the second week in December, and peace descended once more on Treetops. Noël moved into the reconstructed library. The bed pulled smoothly down from the wall between the book-cases. Noël noticed with amusement that Eddie had made it a double bed. 'My friends are ever hopeful,' he thought. Two cupboard doors opened on a small sink and draining-board, with shelves above. The rest of the room was light and spacious, with a sofa and armchairs, and a desk by the window. 'Everything a chap could want,' he thought. Then he thought again. 'Almost.'

Although Mike had been booked in to the retirement home at Whitby for a month, Noël couldn't wait to bring him home, so he rang and made arrangements to pick him up the next day. Mike's room was unchanged but there was still a lot of dust about, so Noël got to work on it.

In the afternoon he took the bus into town and walked down past the Cathedral to the canal and along the bank. Archimedes looked welcoming with her bright curtains and he knocked on the window. An arm waved him on board and he stepped down into the cosy saloon. Beth was feeding one of the twins. A coloured quilt lay on the floor and the other twin was curled up asleep in his tiny sleeping-suit, looking like a small elf. Noël wedged himself into a corner seat and watched Beth. Her earth-mother figure and bare rounded breast made his heart, or his stomach (he wasn't sure which) clench with a deep warm convulsion. No it wasn't desire, it was something far deeper. The tiny boy stopped sucking and his head dropped back on to Beth's cupped hand. A drop of milk hung from her nipple. Beth looked up and smiled.

'Good isn't it?' she said. 'Aren't I lucky?'

'They are the lucky ones,' said Noël. You're a beautiful mother, Beth.'

The babies were usually referred to as 'the twins' but they had been named Benjamin and William, after their respective grandfathers.

'As soon as we decided on their names some wise guy had to call them Bill and Ben,' Eddie had complained, but it was too late. Bill and Ben it was for ever more. They were not identical, but still very difficult to tell apart, unless you were their parents of course, or Margot.

'Bill is my fav'rit,' she confided to Noël once. 'But that's today. Ben'll be fav'rit tomorrow.' Margot was out at the allotment with Eddie today, so Noël and Beth and the twins were able to enjoy the gentle rocking of the boat and the winter silence outside. Beth touched her nipple with a tissue, and tucked her breast away. She put Ben over her shoulder and patted his back for a while, then laid him beside his brother on the floor.

'Can I make you some tea?' asked Noël.

'That would be lovely,' said Beth, and she leaned back comfortably on the cushions.

As Noël pottered about in his old galley he found himself thinking about breasts. He wondered what Hilary's breasts looked like. She was so boyish in her manner, but she definitely had breasts. Now this was an interesting thought...

'Eddie will be coming up to Treetops tomorrow morning,' called Beth. 'He wants to start on those trees.'

'Oh good,' said Noël.

The breasts faded, for the time being.

The next morning Eddie was in the garden chopping up logs. They had worked out that only three of the big pine trees would have to go. This would make space for a pretty large vegetable garden.

'We'll have enough wood here for several winters,' said Eddie, leaning on his log-splitter. 'If we get a decent summer next year they'll burn really well. I was thinking of getting Craig up to give me a hand with the garden. Remember he said he'd do anything? Working out in the fresh air would be really good for him.'

They went into the front hall together and Eddie took off his boots. Although the walls were bare plaster it was beginning to take on the welcoming look that they had all wanted.

'I'll bring coffee out here,' said Noël. 'We can give it a try.'

They sat side by side on some chairs that were still draped in dust-sheets. Light poured in through the new windows and some wintry sunshine gradually outlined shadows on the dusty floor. Noël told Eddie about his recent visit to the newspaper office.

'A lot of fun as ever,' he said, 'but I need somewhere really quiet to work for at least a couple of mornings a week.

It seemed ridiculous to be looking for somewhere to work when you live in an enormous house, but Noël's inner voice wouldn't let him change his mind about this. He'd been offered more use of his 'hot-desk' at the newspaper office, but much as he enjoyed the company it wasn't the right answer just now. The solitude at the Stationmaster's Office had allowed his brain to work clearly. He needed that sort of mental space. New problems were bound to come up as Mike got older. He didn't want to blunder carelessly into unsuitable solutions.

'I've been thinking about that,' said Eddie. 'A bit of an idea came up, but I need to talk to a pal about it.'

'What's the idea?'

'Well you know this 'bedroom tax' that the government has just dreamt up? Well a couple of friends are in a house with a spare room. They're both on benefits, and facing cuts that will be hard to take. Jake has problems which makes it very difficult for him to find paid work. His brother Ivor works part-time but earns very little. They are in a bit of a state about it. I just wondered whether having someone using the room part-time, and paying a bit for it, might get them out of a fix.'

'Wouldn't that affect their welfare benefit though?'

'Not sure,' said Eddie. 'We'd need to look into that. There may be other ways of doing it.'

'I don't want to do anything shady.'

'No, I don't mean that. For instance they are both vegetarians. If you gave them a big box of veg each week, that would save them quite a bit of outlay. We can't grow all the stuff ourselves yet, but we could buy some in. Later we could probably do most it ourselves.'

'Now that's a candidate for the right-hand column!' said Noël. He told Eddie about his List. 'Left-hand column - problems. Right-hand column - intelligent and creative solutions. They seem to arrive out of thin air!'

A week later Eddie and Noël went into town and found the small housing estate where Jake and Ivor lived. Ivor opened the door and gave them a grin. He was tall and extremely thin. His T-shirt hung loosely from his shoulders and flapped over his narrow black jeans. His trainers were worn and fraying at the toes.

'Come on in,' he said. 'Come and meet Jake.'

Jake was in the kitchen. He was sitting at the table and looked up with shining blue eyes in a round rosy face. Noël could see he had Down's Syndrome.

'Jake goes to a workshop most mornings,' said Ivor.

'Yes!' beamed Jake. 'We make lovely coloured things.'

'It's a re-use centre run by Quakers,' continued Ivor. 'They teach people how to make useful things out of waste materials. Jake's working on a rug for our sitting-room.'

'Lovely bright colours,' beamed Jake. 'For in front of the fire.'

'I'm part-time at Tesco's,' continued Ivor. 'Shelf-stacking and suchlike. Not much of a job for a chap with a degree, but it's all I can find just now.'

'What's your degree in?' asked Noël.

'Sociology,' said Ivor. 'It sounds useful, but nobody seems to want me at the moment. Anyway it's better to work than not. Keeps your people-skills active.'

'What sort of skills are those?' asked Noël laughing.

'Sorting out fights. Misunderstandings. Getting people to see both sides of arguments. That sort of thing. You learn more about that at Tesco's than in any University!'

They went up to see the spare room. It was at the back of the house overlooking a school playing-field. At the moment it was full of assorted bits of furniture, boxes and bundles.

'All that lot's going next weekend,' said Ivor. 'I've been collecting stuff for the next Give or Take Day in town. You'd be amazed what people find useful. If you take the room then someone else can have a turn at being the collecting point. I wouldn't be sorry!'

'All I really need is a table and chair' said Noël. 'And a comfortable armchair for thinking in! Maybe an electric kettle for coffee.'

'I could probably pick all those up at the Give or Take next Sunday,' said Ivor, 'if you're not too fussy about colour and design that is.'

The weekly vegetable box had immediately appealed to Ivor. Although he managed to pick up a fair amount at Tesco's from the out-of-date bins he much preferred fresh vegetables to packaged stuff, and he would know how they had been grown.

'I resent paying for pretty pictures, cardboard and plastic,' said Ivor. 'Give me real food any day. It cuts out waste too. We won't be filling our bins.'

'Lots of soup,' said Jake delightedly. 'I love soup.'

'It's good cooking for Jake,' said Ivor. 'No matter what a mess I make of it he still enjoys it.'

'Ivor's a very good cook,' said Jake loyally, and stood up to give him a hug.

Noël was beginning to see parallels between his life and Ivor's.

'Now don't get too involved in this couple,' warned his inner voice. 'You're coming here to work remember.'

'Just for once I think I'll be the best judge of that,' said Noël firmly in reply. 'They won't be here when I'm working, but if we meet up at other times I'm sure we could swap some good ideas.'

Noël didn't tell his colleagues at the office much about his new arrangements. He just said he'd found a small work-space in town and left it at that. He could just imagine Blodwen's oratorio on the subject and he didn't want to have to deal with it.

'Jim's just been here,' said Mike when Noël got home. 'He's going to take me to a lunchtime concert at the Cathedral.'

'That's great. Who's playing?'

'It's a young string trio. They're doing Haydn, Schubert and something else I can't remember.'

Noël went into the library with a large square canvas bag that he had been given at a farmer's market. Into it went his laptop, coffee equipment, notebooks. Yes, they all fitted and there was room for review material and the odd reference book. This would be the Work Bag. Anything that came up could be dropped into it ready for work mornings. That left home life free from trying to do two things at once, unless it was an emergency. His mind felt clear and competent.

'Let's go out Mike,' he said. 'A quick zoom over to Brimham Rocks?' When had he last felt spontaneous like this?

'Great idea!'

'Hmm!' said the inner voice approvingly. 'You're a good learner!'

26. Peter

'Is that Noël? It's Jean here. Are you coming in this afternoon?'

'Yes I am. What's up?'

'Are you coming on the bus or by car?'

'By car today. I need to get back quickly after the meeting.'

'Good. We're a bit worried about Peter. He's been very odd recently. Saying even less than usual. Yesterday he was working on a piece that he promised to send in this morning, but it hasn't come, and it's urgent. We can't contact him. We've tried phone, mobile and email but he's not answering. Could you call in at his house on the way?'

'I've no idea where he lives,' said Noël. 'He's so private he seems to appear and disappear out of thin air.'

'He lives at Huby, which is on your way in, just off the A61. His address is 3 Rigton Lane.'

'Well, I never knew he was so close. I'll certainly call in. I could offer him a lift to the meeting if he's OK to come. We could have been sharing lifts for years.'

Mike was out with Jim at Ripon Cathedral. The lunchtime concert was to be followed by coffee and sandwiches so Noël was free to set off early.

Huby is a small village and it was easy to find Peter's house. It was at the end of a short terrace of stone cottages. It had a small front garden which looked a bit dishevelled. This was surprising as Peter was usually so meticulous. Noël went up the front path, his raincoat brushing against the tall stems each side, and knocked at the door. There was no answer, but he could hear some sounds inside. He knocked again a bit louder. The sounds got louder as if someone had opened an inner door.

'Come round the back.'

It was Peter's voice and he sounded frantic. Noël picked his way across the garden to a small wooden gate and pushed it open. A mossy path led round the side of the cottage to the back door. Noël pushed it open.

'Thank God it's you!' gasped Peter. He was standing with his legs apart and his arms out-stretched. Behind him Noël could see a woman kneeling on the floor. Around her was a spreading pool of milk. 'Please Noël could you phone the doctor for me. I daren't leave her. Tell him that Felicity has taken some sort of overdose – a mixture of her usual pills and something else, not sure what. She's gone over the edge.'

'The wolves are running, the wolves are running,' moaned Felicity behind him. She stood up and took the teapot off the table and began slowly pouring dark tea into the pool of milk. She seemed transfixed by the gradually changing colour.

'She keeps trying to get at the kitchen knives,' whispered Peter. 'That's why I daren't leave her even for a second. Thank goodness you came. How did you know?'

'I didn't even know where you lived,' said Noël. 'The office asked me to call in to remind you about your piece for the paper, and told me where to come.'

'I heard the phone go several times but I couldn't answer it,' said Peter. 'And my mobile's upstairs in my jacket pocket.'

Felicity was still pouring and weeping softly. Suddenly she looked up and saw Noël.

'You!' she shouted. 'You tell me. He can't tell me. What colour is electricity?'

Noël thought for a moment, then whispered to Peter.

'You go and phone. We'll have a talk.'

Peter looked doubtful, but gradually moved sideways and Noël stepped forward.

'Hi Felicity,' he began. 'You know I've always wondered myself what colour electricity is. I've a feeling it is a sort of bright blue, but it just might be white. What do you think?'

Felicity looked curiously at him. She let the teapot drop and it shattered at her feet. She looked down at the pieces and began to wail.

'Don't worry about the teapot,' said Noël. I can see you've got another one on the shelf. A blue one. I think I like the blue one better than the brown one you dropped.'

Noël could hear Peter talking softly on the telephone in the next room. He searched for something else to say.

'They do say that milk is good for cleaning vinyl,' he tried eventually. 'Shall I try to clean up a bit?'

Felicity lunged towards him. He caught her wrists and breathed deeply.

'Do you like dancing?' he asked. 'Shall we try a bit of a dance?' He hummed a tune and her arms relaxed and dropped to her side. 'That's good. Now let's sit down at the table. We haven't met before and I would like to get to know you.' He led her to the table. There was a bowl of cereal overflowing with milk. She sat down with a bump on a chair and her head fell forward into the bowl, knocking it sideways. Cereal and milk flowed off the edge of the table and trickled to the floor.

Peter came back into the kitchen looking relieved, and sat at the other side of the table.

'They're coming,' he said softly.

'The wolves are running, the wolves are running,' cried Felicity again and jumped to her feet.

'Yes, it's exciting when the wolves run by,' said Noël. 'They won't come in here though. They are on their way to the forest.' Noël had absolutely no idea where his words were coming from or what he would be saying next. All he knew was that the best thing to do was to keep talking. It seemed to take Felicity's attention.

It was a good half-hour before the doctor arrived. She carried a small bag and had a young man with her. By this time Noël and Peter had persuaded Felicity into the sitting-room. Her face was streaked with black as she had thrust her hands up the chimney to find some threatening monster and had then cried some more and rubbed her eyes. The doctor talked to her gently and tried to get her to sit down, but Felicity was on her guard. Noël stepped forward again.

'Peter, did I tell you that Felicity and I were dancing in the kitchen? She's a good dancer. We'll show you.' He took her hands and hummed a waltz. Her stance softened and she looked searchingly into his face. The doctor quietly slipped behind her. In a moment or two Felicity relaxed and, very gradually slipped to the floor. The doctor arranged her in the recovery position on the hearth-rug.

'Phew!' said Peter. 'That was good.'

'We've done this before haven't we?' said the doctor. 'But not for a long time. I thought she was doing so well.'

'She's been very unsettled over the last few weeks, so I thought another crisis might be coming,' said Peter. 'It's hospital now I suppose?'

'Yes, the ambulance is on its way,' said the doctor. I must dash off, but Michael here will stay and go with her. He's a psychiatric nurse from the hospital and knows what to do.'

'I'll tell the office you can't come in as your wife's not well,' suggested Noël. 'If you can just email that piece in they should be happy. Then you can sort out the kitchen.'

'I don't want them to know about this,' said Peter desperately. 'It's my problem and I don't want it discussed.'

'Understood,' said Noël. 'Trust me to avoid getting it Blodwenned! I'll give you a ring later and see how things are going.'

It was a short meeting at the office. Noël's explanation that Peter's wife had been taken ill seemed to satisfy their curiosity. He rang Peter on his mobile on the way home.

'Are you OK? Shall I call in on the way back?'

'No I'm fine. I'll be going to see Felicity this evening and need to pick up some shopping. I can't thank you enough for your help.'

'It was certainly a bit unusual!' said Noël. 'Going along with her fantasies seemed to work though. It seemed to catch her interest for a bit. Maybe I'm a fiction writer after all! How long do you think she'll be kept in?'

'It will be some time. They need to get her back to as near normal as possible, and then get her taking control of her own medication. Last time something like this happened it took about four months.'

'When we've got the house a bit more organised you must come over,' said Noël, surprising himself. He had never felt any particular bond with Peter. 'We'll have a spare room if you'd like to stay.'

'That would be good,' said Peter. 'It's such a relief to be able to talk to someone about this. I never have. We don't have many friends as you can imagine.'

Noël wanted to talk to Beth and Eddie about his day, but resolved to keep his promise. They were the sort who would understand completely. In their opinion the world had gone so badly wrong that it wasn't surprising if people were alienated or depressed. 'How to face the Mess we're in Without Going Crazy' Noël remembered. People were amazingly sane on the whole.

27. Nearly Ready

Mike had enjoyed the lunchtime concert. It was a while since they had been to hear live music and it had revived his spirits greatly.

'Such great kids,' he bubbled. 'Only just out of college but playing like real pros. We were up in the choir of the Cathedral so we could be near them. Brilliant acoustic.'

'I wish I'd been there,' said Noël, and he meant it. His visit to Peter had had a delayed effect and he was feeling quite weak and shaky. He sat at the kitchen table with a mug of coffee laced with a large shot of brandy.

'They played a Françaix trio,' went on Mike. 'It has B.A.C.H. backwards in it, and a waltz and a can-can.'

'Not what you'd expect in a Cathedral,' laughed Noël.

'God loved it!' said Mike confidently. 'You know what they say: when God visits the angels they play Bach. When he's gone they play Mozart, and God listens at the keyhole. God knows a good tune when he hears one!'

'We could go over to Manchester and hear the Hallé sometime,' said Noël. He had wanted to suggest this for some time, but didn't know how Mike would take it. Mike's high spirits gave him the courage.

'That would be great Noley. Let's do that.'

'We'll see what's on after Christmas,' said Noël.

Christmas was only two days away. This year they had resolved to keep it simple. 'Just a normal day, with Christmas pudding,' Noël had said. There was still a lot to do in the house and Beth and Eddie would be moving in soon after. They had decided to have a low-key Christmas too, their last on the boat. They had found a buyer for Archimedes. Graham Farr was an artist who spent half his life travelling the world, on foot and public transport and doing sketches, and the rest of his time making paintings of what he had seen. Fortunately he was a miniaturist, so wouldn't need much space for his work, which he sold at galleries, fairs and festivals during the summer months.

'Another free spirit,' commented Noël. 'That's just what Archimedes likes.'

Eddie and Beth had not wanted to inherit, and eventually own, Treetops, as Noël had first suggested. After much discussion they had decided to form a Trust, so that the house could eventually become a home for others who needed it. Noël, Eddie, Beth and Jim were the founding trustees and together would decide the use of the house in the future. Noël had always felt guilty that his great-grandfather had accumulated so much wealth through the work of local miners. He had inherited the house and its land which was far beyond what he needed, but his life had been so active that he hadn't given much thought to the future. Forming a Trust took care of it nicely.

Noël and Mike took a trip to Northallerton to visit a department store of the old-fashioned sort. There was a large range of stock, and the assistants were polite and knowledgeable. Mike hadn't had any new clothes for years, and he wanted to look good for his visit to the Bridgewater Hall. The men's department had a bewildering amount of choice and they were both at a loss as to where to start.

'Can I help you sir?' asked a smiling young man. Noël couldn't remember when he was last called 'sir' and it came as a bit of a shock, but the smile was sincere and friendly.

'My friend here could do with some new trousers, a light jacket and a couple of shirts,' said Noël. 'He can't wander around though, so if you could make some suggestions it would be a great help.'

'Certainly. I'll just take some measurements and then if you would like to sit here I'll see what I can find.'

Mike was installed in a comfortable leather armchair, and various garments were brought for his inspection. The assistant quickly worked out what Mike liked from his reactions.

'That's not me!' said Mike when some thick corduroys were displayed. 'Something soft and smooth would be nice.' He ended up with some moleskin trousers, a racy shirt in pastel stripes and a suede jacket. The bill was large, but the quality was good and they would probably last him for the rest of his life.

'We'll need to shorten the trousers for you,' said the assistant. 'Actually one of your legs is a quarter of an inch shorter than the other I notice.'

'That will be because of his stroke,' said Noël, 'but nobody has ever mentioned that before.'

'It's our job!' said the assistant, laughing. 'We'll make them fit perfectly for you sir. Will you come back next week or shall we send them on?'

It was with a feeling of warm well-being that they drove back to Ripon. Never had the ordeal of shopping for clothes been so pleasant. Noël had splashed out on a new shirt and jersey too.

'This lot will last us the next ten years,' he said, but Mike was quite keen to go back fairly soon for some summer gear, as he called it. He'd enjoyed the personal attention.

'I'd quite like a ....' Mike got stuck. 'You know, to keep the sun off.'

'Hat?'

'Yes, a light grassy thing.'

'A straw hat?'

'That's it. To sit in the garden watching him work!'

'Him?'

'You know, the twins' father.'

'Eddie you mean?'

'Of course I mean Eddie!'

Mike was beginning to find it increasingly difficult to remember certain words. There seemed to be no pattern to it. He forgot people's names very often, but then so do most people. It was quite random nouns that seemed to evade him. He usually found a way of saying what was in his mind in some way, often quite poetically.

The trip to hear the Hallé in Manchester wasn't easy. Parking was difficult, and they had eventually got into the hall rather flustered. Fortunately they had allowed plenty of time, so they could sit in the café bar and calm down. Noël had contacted Stefan and one or two other players who had known Mike. Stefan had almost flattened Mike with his embrace, in fact Mike had disappeared inside his massive arms. Other players stopped for a welcoming word on their way in, and agreed to meet after the show at the usual pub, opposite the artists' entrance.

Noël had booked seats in the front row of the circle so they could have the best possible view of the orchestra. The mish-mash of orchestral sounds died down as the first oboe sounded the A for tuning. Noël took a quick look at Mike. That had been his job of course. How would he be feeling?

'Perfect!' whispered Mike. 'Like a, like a – like a snowdrop!'

Yes, the oboe called through the wash of noise, pure and bright. Mike had found a good word.

The concert began with the overture to Prince Igor. Noël felt Mike tense up as the horn solo wound its way towards the top note. They had both heard many horn players miss that one! Tonight it rang clear and heroic.

'That horn player is just a young girl,' said Mike admiringly through the applause. Things had changed a lot since he had first joined the Hallé.

Sibelius's 'En Saga' was next. It is not often played, and the story that the music tells is not known. The violin parts, Noël had noticed when he had Googled the score the day before, looked like elaborate lacy wall-paper. It had a compelling onward movement and a strong climax before it died away.

'That's not done often,' said Mike. 'It's a bit long!'

After the interval it was Tchaikovsky's Symphony No.6, the 'Pathétique'. Stefan's warm bassoon sound crept into the hall against the almost inaudible double-basses, setting the mood of loss and desolation. After the third movement, which ends with a massive climax, a few of the audience applauded excitedly as they often do, thinking the work had reached a triumphant conclusion. The fourth movement, with its hollowed-out emotions, led down to lonely depths by Stefan, faded away into nothingness. The audience was still for several seconds before they could bring themselves to clap. Tears were pouring down Mike's face.

'I miss her,' he whispered.

Noël leaned towards him.

'I miss Mary so much. I miss her smile, and her – and her – and her body-nice.'

Noël reached out and gave Mike's shoulder a squeeze. They stayed in their seats until most of the circle had emptied.

After a happy time with members of the wind section in *The Briton's Protection*, Noël and Mike drove home through the darkness. The threatened snow had not yet arrived and the sky was clear. Noël looked at the stars and pondered the new expression 'body-nice' that Mike had invented. How long was it since he had experienced any body-nice? More than fifteen years. Even longer since anyone who really mattered had made him feel physically treasured and loved. Most of the time it didn't seem to matter, he was fully occupied with managing his life, and managing Mike's life too. It was like living for two, and Mike's well-being and safety had to take priority.

He had come back from his week in the Stationmaster's Office feeling calm and rested, and ready to cope cheerfully with all that life might throw at him. Now he was beginning to feel the stress of constant awareness building up again. Beth had, as usual, noticed how he was feeling.

'Conference needed! Can you come down to the boat for lunch? It will be the last time before we move in and there are one or two things to sort out.'

Noël wondered what they might be and hoped nothing serious had cropped up to ruin their plans. He left a picnic lunch for Mike, and asked Kay if she could call in to make sure he was OK.

'Of course,' Kay had said. 'I enjoy his company. I'll bring my patchwork and stay for a while. Take your time.'

Eddie and Margot had gone off to play on the swings in the park. Margot didn't seem to feel the cold at all. Life on the boat with so much fresh air had made her a strong and healthy little girl. The twins were gurgling happily on their play-mat. It never ceased to amaze Noël how calm and contented this little family was. He had said as much to Eddie one day when he was taking a break from the garden.

'I think it's because we always talk about things,' said Eddie. 'If something upsets one of us, or there's a disagreement, we fix a time to talk about it. Then we don't give up until we've found a solution that we're both happy with.'

'Politicians could learn a lot from you two!' laughed Noël. This was why he was slightly anxious about this lunchtime call. Was there something serious they needed to sort out?

'Now then,' said Beth when, after some tasty soup, they were settled with their mugs of coffee. 'How is The List going?'

'You mean my Problems and Solutions List? It's going quite well on the whole. It only breaks down if I'm tired. Like today in fact – we had rather a disturbed night. Mike couldn't sleep and wandered out into the hall. I heard him humming and tapping about with his stick so I went to see what was up. There didn't seem to be anything in particular on his mind. I made a cup of tea for us both and then he settled down again.'

93

'Just like the twins!' said Beth. 'There's nothing like a warm drink for making them settled down.'

'Then this morning I'm afraid I lost my cool a bit.'

'Why was that?'

'Oh I saw Mike sitting staring at a small piece of paper in his hand. Nothing unusual in that but he was still doing it an hour later. I went to see what it was and he was examining the bill from our shopping expedition.

'I don't understand,' said Mike.

'What don't you understand?'

'There are four things on this bill, but I can only find three new things in the wardrobe.'

'That's because we left the trousers to be shortened,' explained Noël.

'There's two for £35, one for £75 and one for £120,' Mike went on.

'That's right,' said Noël.

'So where's the fourth thing?'

'Still at the shop,' said Noël, getting impatient.

'What shop?'

'In Northallerton, you remember – we went there…'

'But why are there only three?' complained Mike.

'Oh for heaven's sake Mike!' shouted Noël. 'Think!'

Not only was he too tired to think of a better way of explaining, but he felt fear too. Was Mike losing his mind? How would he cope if Mike lost it completely?

'In the end I managed to divert him,' Noël explained to Beth. 'I suggested we went into my room to check my purchases. He put the bill down on the table and came like a lamb. I showed him my new shirt and jersey. Then we went into the kitchen and had another cup of tea. I slipped back into his room and tidied the bill away into his desk drawer. I feel dreadful about shouting at him though.'

'Conference open!' said Beth. 'Subject for discussion: your sanity.'

'What?' shouted Noël. '*My* sanity?'

'Hush! You'll wake the twins.' Ben (or Bill) gave a moan and started to whimper. Beth leaned down and stroked his back, and his thumb went comfortingly into his mouth.

'Even at that age they understand anger,' said Beth. 'Now let's talk a bit quieter. To manage caring for Mike you need to be in top condition. I know you are very fond of him but you are also human and need some time to yourself.'

'I sometimes wonder whether I'm living my life or his,' agreed Noël. 'I wouldn't have it any different though. I'm glad he came to live with me. No regrets.'

'No regrets of course, but there's a need for a lot of strength and patience. You need to re-charge your batteries regularly.'

'The mornings working at Ivor's are good for that,' said Noël. 'I can think clearly and write well there.'

'That's work though,' continued Beth. 'You need time to wander, smell some flowers, have no deadlines, read a novel, take a boat out…'

'Oh yes! I miss the boat a lot, and the freedom. But I still don't regret what I did,' he added defensively.

'I've taken the liberty of ringing Robin Hill Lodge,' continued Beth calmly. 'They are able to book respite weeks in advance. I suggest you don't wait until you're at shouting pitch but reserve several weeks spaced out over the rest of the year.'

'That's like farming out my responsibilities,' said Noël indignantly. 'How do I know that I'll really need those weeks? Things might be going really well...'

'Believe me you will need them, and you will benefit from them,' said Beth firmly. 'Remember how good you felt after your last break?'

'True.' Noël had to admit she was right, as usual.

'Mike isn't your property,' she went on seriously. 'He needs to be part of the wider world as much as possible. That's already happening in some ways with more people coming to the house. You need to build on it. Have you talked to Carer's Support again?'

'No. I didn't feel the need to,' said Noël stubbornly.

'Well do,' said Beth. 'Ask them if they have a volunteer who could take Mike out sometimes.'

'That's really not necessary. I can take him out myself.'

'You're missing the point again!'

'Oh yes. Variety of experience?'

'Got it. End of conference.'

Noël decided to walk home rather than taking the bus. Kay would be with Mike, and that would be a nice change from a shouty music journalist. He paused in the market-place and took out his mobile phone.

'Ripon Carer's Support. Annie speaking. Can I help you?'

'May I call in at your office sometime? I would like to see whether you could find a volunteer to take my disabled friend out sometimes.'

Annie remembered Noël as she had been the person who made the initial assessment. She had been wondering how they were getting on. She recalled that Noël had been a bit tight-lipped.

'You can call in now if you're free. Someone has just cancelled.'

Noël rang Kay to let her know what was happening and then made his way to the Carer's Support office. He carefully worked out his speech as he went. No, he wasn't pleading weakly for help. He wanted to widen Mike's experience of life. That was it. Different voices, different interests. He had it all nicely worked out by the time he rang the bell.

A young woman with long dark hair opened the door.

'My name's Noël Burke – I rang a little while ago.'

'Oh yes. Annie's on the phone just now. Please come in, she won't be long.'

Noël was shown into a small room with two comfortable chairs and a table. He could hear a voice speaking calmly in the next room. 'Don't worry Janet. We all do it! Barbara will be round tomorrow to take your Mum out for an hour or two. Don't blame yourself now. Promise?'

Annie came into the room smiling and held out her hand. She had fair hair which Noël remembered had hung like a curtain around her small features. Today she had it in plaits and wore candy-striped trousers. Noël did his prepared speech quite well, but then his guilt swept over him.

'I'm afraid I shouted at him this morning. It wasn't good.'

Annie laughed. 'You wouldn't be normal if you didn't shout sometimes. I'm sure it isn't the first time in his life he's been shouted at.'

'No that's true!' said Noël. 'Some conductors at the Hallé went in for quite a lot of shouting. Mike used to say that those with the least talent made the most noise.'

'Oh yes, Mike's a retired musician. I remember now. I wonder whether Gerald is interested in music.'

'Who's Gerald?'

'He's a retired geography teacher. He retired early, rather disillusioned with the way education's going. He's decided to take up nature photography instead. He came in to offer us some volunteering time last week.'

'Mike loves being out in the countryside,' said Noël. 'We don't do it often enough. He can't walk far but it always does him good to get out of town.'

'How often would you like someone to take Mike out?'

'Well, I'm still working part-time. Three mornings a week, with occasional afternoon meetings in the office in Leeds. Mike gets up pretty late though, and the Leeds meetings are unpredictable.'

'Instead of him going out while you're working, why not arrange it for when you are free? That would benefit you more. You could please yourself for a while.'

'That's a thought!' said Noël. 'My neighbours often look in on him when I'm working anyway. I wonder what Mike would think though. Wouldn't he think I didn't enjoy his company?'

'You need some time to yourself. That's what's important. Gerald also feels the need to give his time to someone other than himself. He's lost his wife, so lives on his own. You'd be doing him a favour.'

'Perhaps they wouldn't like each other,' said Noël.

'We'd arrange an informal meeting first,' said Annie. 'Maybe more than one, if necessary. Take it from there?'

Noël went home feeling light on his feet. Gerald would be joining them for coffee the following week.

Now that the entrance hall at Treetops was a light, cheerful meeting-place, and the builders had got rid of all the draughts, 'morning coffee in the hall' was a regular event. On the days when Noël wasn't working he and Mike never knew who might appear. Cecil and Emily had driven over from York and exclaimed with delight when they saw the transformation. The wood-burner was throwing out a red glow, the pale rush-matting reflected the winter sunshine. The sofa and armchairs, rescued from a particularly fruitful Give or Take event, were grouped together with colourful rugs thrown over them. The staircase curved up behind, with the small house-lift tucked discreetly behind.

It was while Cecil and Emily were there that Noël first mentioned Gerald.

'There's this chap Gerald I've heard about,' he said. 'He's retired from teaching and living on his own. His wife has died and he's looking for things to do.'

'Poor chap,' said Mike. 'My wife died you know. In 2008.' Noël was amazed at how accurately Mike could remember certain facts, while others seemed to fall straight out of his head.

'Gerald is hoping to find people who would like to go out exploring the Dales with him,' went on Noël. 'He's taking up photography quite seriously, and there are so many amazing places around here.'

'He could go to Brimham Rocks,' said Mike. 'We went there once didn't we Noley? Couldn't believe the shapes.' Again Noël wondered at Mike's recall. How could his brain be so spasmodic?

'Would you like to go with him?' asked Noël. He felt rather uncomfortable at engineering Mike in this way, but it did seem to be happening fairly naturally.

'Yes I'd like that,' said Mike. Noël held his breath and counted up to ten, slowly. Would Mike insist that Noël went too? He hadn't an answer ready for that. Things had moved too quickly.

'I think Gerald would be pleased to find someone to go with,' Noël said finally. 'He's coming over next week. We can ask him.'

'Good,' said Mike.

'Very good!' said Noël.

28. Moving in

'Sounds like a bloody hotel,' roared Blodwen. 'Fawlty Towers' isn't in it. Have you found a Manuel?'

Noël held his breath. Noël often held his breath these days. It sometimes worked.

'I'm the major domo,' he replied, preening himself and flicking back his hair. 'I won't need an assistant. Anyway we're getting a dog.'

'What sort of dog?' asked Peter. He was back at work and looking somewhat better than when they had last seen him.

'Golden retriever I think,' said Noël. 'Hilary's the dog expert.'

'Who's this Hilary? Is he moving in as well?' called Blodwen from the doorway.

'Hilary's the architect. He's a she.'

'Oh God here we go!' cried Blodwen. 'Got your sexes mixed up again have you?'

'Not this time. She's rather nice as a matter of fact.'

'Ha!'

Noël perched on a desk and turned over the pile of books that Jean had given him. There were two hefty paperbacks: 'The Moneyless Manifesto' and 'The Ascent of Humanity'.

'Apparently one of these books inspired the other,' said Jean. 'One is by a chap who lived for several years without using money.'

'Bloody scrounger was he?' bellowed Blodwen.

'No, I think he did work for people, and they gave him food and shelter,' said Jean. 'There was a television programme about him some time ago. I can't remember the details. I think the Chief wants a combined feature about the two books. There's another he mentioned which I found second-hand online. Lewis Hyde 'The Gift'. Apparently that ties in too. Over to you Noël!'

'I may be some time…' said Noël, feeling the weight of the books. 'Anything else?'

'Peter is researching local currencies past and present,' went on Jean.

'That's right,' said Peter. 'I understand you've got a LETS group in Ripon. I'd like to interview them.'

'What's LETS?'

'Local Exchange Trading System.' They exchange goods and services for a created currency unit. No money needed. York have units called 'Yorkies' roughly equivalent to a pound.'

'Well money seems to be a bloody dead loss these days,' shouted Blodwen. 'Trillions off-shore and nothing for the poor. Flippin' disgrace. Don't know why there isn't blood on the streets.'

'There may well be if things don't improve.' said Peter.

'I don't know about Ripon LETS,' said Noël, 'but I bet Eddie does. I'll ask him.' He packed the books into his bag and swung it on his shoulder.

'See you in a couple of weeks,' he called. 'By then we'll have a houseful.'

It was a crisp winter day when Beth and Eddie moved in to Treetops. One of Eddie's woodworking colleagues helped them move, using his Transit van. Coming from the boat, with its fitted beds and cupboards, they hadn't much to bring, and soon the upper landing was filled with cardboard boxes and plastic sacks. They had some of Noël's family furniture which they would use until Eddie found time to make things more to their taste.

'Never slept in a carved mahogany bed before,' said Eddie. 'Maybe we'll get used to it!' Noël knew this wasn't the case. Eddie had been studying Quaker furniture and had found simplicity of design that felt absolutely right for him and his family. They used the back staircase, which had originally been for the servants, but had been widened and lightened by Hilary to make a pleasant independent entrance. Noël insisted that they must feel free to come and go through the rejuvenated front hall, but Beth wanted the children to learn to respect Noël and Mike's privacy.

'Can we come down for eleven-o-clockses?' asked Margot.

'Of course!' said Noël. 'That's the idea of eleven-o-clockses. Gathering time!'

The noise of footsteps upstairs, and the occasional cry from the twins, brought the house to life. At first Mike was anxious.

'What's that noise?'

'That will be Margot, running as usual.'

'What's that?'

'Just a door shutting.'

'I can hear a buzzing…'

'That will be the vacuum cleaner. I've lent them ours for the time being.'

'What's that?'

'Just a door shutting again.'

Noël wondered whether the questions would ever stop. If Mike's short-term memory got really bad perhaps he'd *never* learn what the new noises were. Noël felt a surge of tension in his chest. He often felt this these days, as if his gullet was rising and burning his throat. It worried him, but he hadn't consulted a doctor – there was too much to do. He slipped quietly into the kitchen and poured himself a small shot of brandy. That burned his throat too, almost unbearably.

'Calm down, breathe quietly,' said his inner voice, 'and let me tell you now, you're not going down that particular route.'

'What route would that be?' Noël asked innocently, but he knew only too well.

'Using alcohol as a refuge,' said the voice. 'You did that once before. Remember?'

'Oh yes, I remember only too well.'

'Go into the library. Find a notebook. Write down how many days to your respite week. Write down the things you need to do today, then OK – finish the brandy, just this once.'

Noël did as he was told. Ten days to his first respite week. Today he had to ring Hilary to find out about the dog, and also to invite her up to a celebration supper now that the whole project was complete. She had called in a few times since the building work had been completed, not always with a particular reason. He enjoyed her matter-of-fact company. She'd be at work at the moment, so he would send a text.

'Supper soon? Talk dog? Friday good for us.' The answer came back quickly:

'Friday good. Time?'

'7ish?'

'Brill!'

Noël wondered what was happening to the English language. His father would have been appalled at the casual mini-syllable exchange that had replaced a proper invitation. He could see him now, going upstairs to put a tie and sports jacket on when guests were coming, even for an informal visit. Times had changed with exponential speed, and although Noël was more or less keeping up he knew he would soon be outpaced. He tried not to think about getting old.

'Remember old Clive?' he'd said to Mike once. 'Played flute in the Birmingham. He was old before he was thirty!'

'Clive? Mmm. Not sure.'

'He used to worry about his pension and life insurance all the time. Probably since he was at school.'

'Oh old Clive who bought that alto flute?'

'Yes, that's him. He bought the alto to do 'Daphnis & Chloë'. Then he fluffed it at the concert. He was almost suicidal afterwards. I didn't mention it in the crit!'

'That was kind, Noley. You always were a friendly critic. The chaps liked you.'

'Yes, it was nearly all chaps then, wasn't it? Lots of talented young women in orchestras these days. You should see the Northern Sinfonia now – very glamorous!'

'That would be nice,' said Mike. Noël made a mental note. The Northern Sinfonia sometimes played at the Whitby Pavilion, and that was near Robin Hill Lodge. That could work out well.

29. Time Out

Mike was once more installed at Robin Hill Lodge. The staff were delighted to see him again, and he enjoyed their attention. He found his favourite place by the window and looked down on the grey waters of the harbour reflecting the coloured boats.

'Have a good week Noley,' he called cheerfully as Noël, reluctantly, sidled out of the lounge. He still felt bad about this 'respite' arrangement. It seemed to indicate failure of some sort. Nevertheless as he closed the front door behind him and smelt the sea air he could feel his spirits lift and the tension in his shoulders relax.

Mike was safe.

Noël was free.

He had been so tired in recent weeks that he found it difficult to decide what to do with his week. In fact he had found it impossible.

'What would you really love to do?' Beth had asked.

'No idea! Whenever I think of a plan I automatically wonder how Mike will cope with it. Then I remind myself that he doesn't need to. Then I try to think of something that doesn't include him. Then I seize up – I'm so used to thinking for two.'

'Why not just do whatever takes your fancy on the day you drop him off in Whitby?' said Beth. 'If you just stand outside the front door for a while an idea will come. If it didn't you'd just have to stand there for a week!'

'You're right. Something always comes,' said Noël. He remembered being in New York once. He'd taken a yellow-cab up into Harlem to find a music shop.

'Why you wanna go there?' asked the taxi driver. 'There's plenny o' music stores downtown.'

'It's a particular one I've been told about,' said Noël. 'What's the problem?'

'Yeller cabs don't go there,' said the taxi driver. 'Not unless they have to.' He jerked the cab into gear and drove sullenly north. The shop was nothing special after all. 'It must have changed hands,' thought Noël. 'I'll get a cab back downtown.'

He stood on a corner to wait. Derelict buildings stretched away in all directions. Many windows were boarded up, walls blackened by fire. No cabs came past. Looking around Noël noticed that nobody was moving. People stood in silent groups, or alone, leaning on corners. Every face was black. He shifted from one foot to another. A figure in a shabby raincoat emerged from a doorway and crossed the road; the first white face he had seen. She disappeared down a nearby alleyway. To his left there was a subway entrance. It was dark, graffiti-covered and littered with rubbish. No, not a good idea. Noël just stood – he had no idea what to do. A few cars cruised around and a black saloon pulled up beside him.

'Wanna cab?' asked the driver.

'Yes. I'm waiting for a yellow cab.'

'Yeller cabs don't come this place,' said the driver.

'I'll just wait. Thank you.'

Ten more minutes went by. The black saloon had cruised off but came back beside him again.

'This's a cab mister,' said the driver. 'Hop in an' I'll take you. Where you wanna go?'

There just didn't seem to be an alternative, and the driver seemed a kindly character.

'I need to get to the Met. The Metropolitan Opera House,' said Noël.

'Where dat?'

After some thought Noël came up with a street number. His hotel was just around the corner from the Met.

'Midtown. Around 63rd Street.'

'Fine. Hop in.'

The back of the cab had a shaggy pile rug on the back seat which looked as if it had seen many years of use. Noël sat on it gingerly, and kept a careful eye on the direction they were taking. He need not have worried. Charlie, the driver, was full of good jokes and Noël was soon back on familiar territory. Yes, the answer to an impossible problem was often just to stand still and wait.

It had happened in Crete too. Noël had, on impulse, taken a last-minute flight in mid-winter. At Heraklion airport the currency exchange desk was closed. He had no Greek money. What to do? Outside the airport building it was cold and windy, and there were few people about. It reminded him of the New York experience, so he just stood about. Once again it was a taxi-driver who came to the rescue.

'Where you want to go?'

'I want to get into town, but I haven't any Greek money.'

'No problem. I drive you to a cash machine. You draw cash. You pay me!'

Not only that, but the driver took him to a small hotel, run by a cousin of his.

'Good, cheap, very clean,' he assured him. 'Good restaurant round the corner.'

This was the start of a carefree week exploring the island outside the tourist season. One of the best holidays he'd ever had. After a couple of days in Heraklion he'd taken a bus to Spili and spent the following day walking through the mountains, eagles circling above him.

In the evening he stopped at a small village bar and asked if there was somewhere to stay. The barman leaned out of the door.

'Angeleeeeeeeeeeeena!'

A portly lady emerged from her front door further down the street, wiping her hands on her apron. There was a verbal exchange like rapid gunfire and then she waved to him and went back inside.

'Angelina will give you a bed,' said the barman. 'And a supper if you like.'

Noël's Greek was minimal, but with the help of smiles and gestures he had a merry evening with Angelina and her extremely pregnant daughter. He slept fully clothed, as there was no heating in his room. Why would you need heating in Crete? They wouldn't accept any payment the next day, and waved him on with smiles and laughter. The next day he walked on, and as the blue of the Libyan sea came into view his heart was singing.

Now Noël stood outside Robin Hill Lodge, smiling as he remembered Crete. Whitby to Crete was a bit far for just a week. He had enjoyed the freedom of that unplanned holiday. Yes, it was freedom that he needed just now. He opened the car door, reached in for his small ruck-sack, swung it on his shoulder and then locked the car and walked away. The car could stay at Robin Hill too. He was off…

Further along the road there was a cliff-top view of the harbour. Noël leaned on the wall and looked down. A grey curtain descended over his mind as the relentless anxieties of his daily life crowded back into his brain. Mike needed more attention these days. Every week there seemed to be appointments at the health centre, to check on this and that. No doubt that the NHS was doing a thorough job, but checking his INR, checking his mild diabetes, checking his odd aches and pains had meant that Noël was managing fewer of his working mornings uninterrupted. He heard a car running over the cobbles below, like a drum-roll.

'Oh no!' he found himself thinking. 'Not again!' A drum-roll always triggered Mike's favourite story.

'Oh Noley, you know how 'Tombeau de Couperin' starts?'

'Yes. Major oboe solo. Quite scary!'

'That's right. D'you know what happened at the Hallé Proms?'

'Go on…'

'Well, we were starting the concert with Tombeau, but the timpanist thought we were starting with something else. As the conductor's stick came down he did a tremendous roll!'

'Oh dear!'

'But d'you know what? I didn't drop a stitch! Just played the solo as normal. The conductor was so impressed. He wasn't too pleased with the timp player though!'

'Good story Mike!'

Yes it was a good story, but in recent weeks Classic FM had played an unusual number of pieces which started with a drum roll.

Then there was that letter from Stella. His mother had heard about the alterations to Treetops, and the new living arrangements, and she was not pleased. She had the impression that Noël had wrecked the family home and filled it with vagrants.

'You'd better come down and talk to her,' Stella had said. Noël was not looking forward to it.

He looked down over the steep cliff. He was doing his best for everybody, he thought, but he hadn't got endless energy and patience. He missed his freedom badly. He remembered times when he could sit on the deck of Archimedes in the sun and just appreciate what a glorious place the world was. At night he sometimes walked along the tow-path and enjoyed the silence and the stars.

Looking down at the rocks below he found himself considering the solution - a moment of glorious flying freedom and then the peace of oblivion. It was uncannily tempting. He jerked himself away from the wall and started walking. Where could he find some peace? What about The Stationmaster's Office again? At the Public Library he went online and looked it up. Fully booked. He put in today's date and did a search – any cottage anywhere in the UK would do. He just needed some peace.

The 'last minute deals' that came up were somewhat unattractive. A flat in an ugly building in a Northumbrian market town took his eye. No wonder nobody wanted that. He rang the number and arranged to take it from that evening for a week. His feeling of freedom began to return. He decided to go by public transport. It would take him through some new territory and would feel like an adventure. His inner voice, which had been quiet for rather a long time, spoke up.

'Doesn't take much to make you feel adventurous these days!'

'Perhaps this is what getting old is like,' replied Noël gloomily.

'All in the mind!' replied the voice. 'Trouble is your mind is so tensed up that it isn't working.'

'But life's pretty good really. Lovely home. Good friends. Everybody around me is fairly content.'

'Yes, but…'

'I'll talk to you later,' said Noël firmly and set off for the bus station.

By an assortment of buses and trains Noël travelled North. At Newcastle the station was buzzing with police in yellow jackets.

'Big English Defence League anti-Muslim demo,' said the man at the coffee stall with relish. 'After that soldier being killed in Woolwich.' Noël's heart sank. How many Muslims have died at British hands in recent years, he wondered. When would it all stop and people begin to treat each other as fellow human beings, flying through space on this ball of rock. In his travelling days he had lived happily among people of many religions. Most of the world's population seemed to be concerned with their everyday life, their families and friends, their crops and businesses. There would always be a small percentage of aggressive nutters, but life shouldn't be lived in fear of them. It should be lived joyfully in spite of them.

Governments ruled by fear, and were themselves ruled by fear…

'Not now!' said his inner voice. 'Take a break.'

The last lap of the journey was forty minutes by bus on a bumpy road. The holiday flat was reached through an archway off the market place, and up a short flight of stone steps. A key-code let him in to an area of crimson carpet and shiny black furniture. The wind rattled the windows. Road-works lined the street outside but mercifully work had stopped for the night. Noël moved all the artificial flowers and china knick-knacks to the windowsills and then drew the curtains. He put his few belongings on the coffee table, having removed the folder of 'local attractions' and went upstairs to the bedroom. It was under the eaves and surprisingly hot and airless. The sheets were of nylon and the duvet and pillows were lumpy with man-made fibre stuffing.

The owners had left a flowery welcome card, a bottle of red wine and a box of chocolates. Mercifully there was milk in the fridge, and tea and coffee on the kitchen shelves. Noël's supper consisted of a sandwich from Newcastle station, several chocolates and a generous amount of wine. 'That should make me sleep,' he thought as he plodded wearily up the stairs.

The night was spent tossing and turning. First on one side then the other. He was too hot with the duvet on and too cold with it off. His head ached. His stomach rebelled at the wine and chocolates. At four in the morning he went down and made a cup of tea, then returned for another try. Eventually sleep came, fitful and with horrifying dreams. An army of EDL warriors was closing in on Ripon from the south-east, and a band of angry Muslims were converging from the south-west. They were due to meet and clash, and then ravage the town. Margot had given birth to twins, but couldn't bring them home to the safety of Treetops until they had been 'chipped'. All children had a microchip implanted at birth so that the State could keep track of them for life. Noël woke exhausted and fearful that life was not worth living. It took several hours, lying back on the slightly sticky black sofa, to return to something like reality.

The little town had good food shops and a charity shop with a reasonable selection of books. As there were no books in the holiday flat Noël bought half a dozen, and settled down to work his way through them. Detective stories, family sagas and foreign travel took his mind far from the shiny sofa and gradually his mind relaxed. By the end of the week he was taking long walks and sleeping for most of the night. His inner voice was silent.

30. Craig

It was some months since the stone-throwing episode, when Eddie had marched Craig home. Nadine was a frail woman whose husband had disappeared soon after Craig was born. She had been horrified at what Craig had done to Margot, and turned on Craig with her hand raised. Eddie stood behind Craig with his hands on his shoulders.

'No, don't hit him. He's had his punishment and apologised. We need to talk about what caused it. I don't think he's a cruel lad by nature.'

They talked about the bullying at school, but Nadine was nervous about going to complain.

'They might take it out on him if I make a fuss,' she said.

'Bullying needs to be tackled, otherwise the bullies win,' said Eddie. 'Would you like me to come with you?'

'What would people think?' she said nervously. 'They'd think I'd taken up with someone. The gossip round here is terrible.'

'Well think about it,' said Eddie. 'Here's my mobile number. I'd be very happy to put a stop to this for the sake of all the children at the school, not just Craig.'

Nadine thought for a moment.

'Could you pretend to be some sort of official?' she said.

'Mm. Not sure about that,' said Eddie, 'but I could carry a clip-board. You can get anywhere if you carry a clip-board!'

'It would look as if you had a list of complaints,' said Nadine, brightening. 'That would impress them.'

Eddie said he would wait to hear from her. He went off and did some research online and found an organisation called Chandwicks that went into schools specifically to deal with bullying. Their expertise took the pressure off teachers and had some significantly good results. When Nadine contacted him a couple of weeks later he armed himself with Chandwicks' information, collected Nadine brandishing his clip-board, and together they went to meet the head teacher. Eddie didn't pretend to be an official once they were at the school, but his air of assumed authority meant that he was taken seriously. As he suspected the head teacher knew which boys were causing the trouble, but had no idea of the sexual side of their activities.

'There has been an outbreak of "sexting" at the school recently,' he said, 'and we've been clamping down on that as much as is possible. Physical threatening outside school we didn't know about.'

Eddie gave him to understand that something serious needed to be done and offered him the information about Chandwicks. He left Nadine's home address, and his own, and said that they both looked forward to hearing what action the school was taking.

'That was impressive!' said Nadine as they walked back to her house.

'I hope it works, and that Craig will be happier now,' said Eddie. 'What are his best subjects?'

'He's not that good at written work,' said Nadine 'but he's good with his hands and gets on well in Designing Technology or whatever they call it – working with metal and wood and stuff.'

'I need some help with clearing some land, felling and chopping up trees. Would you mind if he came to help some Saturday mornings? I'd take good care he didn't hurt himself – do proper training with the tools. He could feel he was paying back for some of the upset he caused Beth and me.'

Nadine liked this idea. Craig was desperately nervous, but after one morning working alongside Eddie in the fresh cold air on the hill his confidence began to grow.

Margot was very concerned about Craig, and always asked if she could take him a drink and biscuits mid-morning.

'He's not a bad boy,' she insisted the first time he appeared, taking his grimy hand. Craig blushed furiously.

31. Peter again

Peter came into the house through the back door and dropped his car keys on the kitchen table. The house was dark and silent. The kitchen smelt slightly of stale milk. A scattering of soot covered the sitting-room fireplace. He threw himself down on the sofa and was soon asleep, still wearing his outdoor clothes. Almost immediately the telephone shrilled and he leapt up to answer it, staggering against the table.

'Is that Mr Simmonds?'

'Yes, Peter Simmonds here.'

'It's Michael Brent from St Benedict's. I came with the doctor when we collected Felicity. Can you come over to the hospital please?'

'Why? What's happened?'

'Felicity needs some specialist treatment and we need to consult you about it.'

'I'll be right over.'

Peter had a feeling that there was something more behind this request than had been said. He picked up his keys, took a banana from the fruit-bowl and made his way out to the car. St Benedict's was only five miles away at Arthington, a journey he was familiar with. He drove fast, trying not to think.

'She's in here,' said Michael, who had been waiting at the entrance for Peter to arrive. They went into a small side-ward close by and Felicity was there, lying on a trolley, with a nurse standing beside her. Felicity was chalk-white. The nurse shook her head. Peter moved to touch her, but Michael put out a hand to keep him back. Michael leant over the trolley and felt for the pulse in her neck.

'Too late I'm afraid,' he said quietly. 'She's gone.'

Peter stepped forward, put his hand on Felicity's forehead and knew it was true although she was still faintly warm. He sat down on a chair and put his head in his hands.

'She'd been getting on so well,' said Michael, putting a hand on Peter's shoulder. 'We have no idea what triggered this collapse. She was sitting in the patients' lounge. A nurse had recently been on the medication round and said she looked fine. She didn't read or watch television of course, just sat and watched us. We couldn't interest her in anything. She always seemed alert, but not unduly distressed. There will have to be a post-mortem of course.'

'What should I do now?' Peter's shoulders heaved.

'Go home, have a meal and sleep if you can. We'll call you in tomorrow when we know what's happening. Would you like someone to come with you?'

Peter thought about the state of the house and shook his head.

'No, I'll be alright.' He got wearily to his feet and shook Michael's hand. 'Thanks for all you've done for her. Perhaps she's at peace at last.'

When Peter got home he went to the phone and rang Noël's number. No reply. He was about to try his mobile, then dropped the handset on the table. He threw himself face down on the rumpled sofa and began to sob uncontrollably. What made it worse was that he knew that he was sobbing with relief as well as sorrow.

32. Oh Mother!

On the last day of his Northumbrian week Noël had a call from Peter, telling him the news about Felicity. Noël sensed a barely perceptible lift in Peter's voice, and realised what a strain he must have been living under.

'We'll meet up when I get back,' said Noël, 'but I've got to go to Sussex first to visit my mother.'

'Is she OK?'

'Oh yes, she's indestructible. I've just got to go and do some explaining about what's going on at Treetops. She's heard half the story and doesn't see the point.'

'Good luck!'

Noël had decided to get the Sussex trip over as soon as possible and arranged for Mike to have an extra couple of days at Whitby. Mike had been very understanding about it.

'Go and sort her out Noley!' he'd said cheerily. 'Tell her what a wonderful place Treetops is.'

'I'd better not be too enthusiastic about it or she might want to come and join us!'

'Oops! Tread carefully!'

'Will do. See you Wednesday.'

Noël re-packed his small bag, this time including the DVD 'Ancient Futures: Learning from Ladakh' which had made such an impression on him. The week away had done him good and he felt ready to tackle Mother. He took trains from Leeds to Lewes and Stella met him at the station.

'I've got to go out this evening,' said Stella. 'WI meeting, and I'm the chair.'

'You *are* getting respectable!' laughed Noël.

'You can have Mother to yourself,' went on Stella. 'She'll take some convincing, but you've more chance if I'm out of the way.'

They had a cheerful supper together, then Stella bustled off leaving Noël and his mother facing each other across the fireplace in the sitting-room.

'Now Noël,' began Mother 'what on earth have you been doing?'

'Before I start talking about it I'd like you to watch a film with me,' said Noël.

'A Film?'

'Yes. It's a documentary about a region in the north of India.'

'What's that got to do with Treetops?'

'Quite a lot actually.'

Noël turned the lights down and moved across to sit beside his mother as the film began. At first she was restless and kept adjusting her cardigan and sensible skirt. Gradually the smiling faces, the music and the spectacular landscapes began to capture her attention and she sat back and relaxed a little. When it was over she turned to face him.

'What dreadful things have happened to those happy people,' she said. 'And all in just a few years.'

'Yes, and all those things have also happened to us over the last half-century or so, but more slowly. We've barely noticed the changes. We only gradually realise that people no longer help each other freely, have come to rely on goods from thousands of miles away, buy commercially produced food, have lost the skills to make and do for themselves. Worst of all people are lonely, separated from each other. Old and sick people are shut away.'

'At least I haven't been shut away!'

Noël sighed. Mother always clinched any discussion by referring it back to herself. It was safer to stop thinking about those awful far-away things. Noël gathered his thoughts carefully.

'My friend Mike was shut away. I couldn't bear that. He's such a lively, loving person.'

'But it wasn't your job to look after him. I thought he had a son. He and his wife should be looking after him.'

'His son isn't married. He works in Africa for an oil company. Mike couldn't live safely there, nor would he want to. They share no interests. Mike and I have a lot in common – music and boats for a start. Maybe he's the brother I didn't have!'

'Hm!' said Mother, wondering if this was a criticism of her child-bearing prowess. No. Two was enough. She shrugged. 'What about these other people?'

'Beth and Eddie are young, energetic and wise. They have taught me a lot about living well. As you could see in Ladakh it's good for different generations to live together. The very old and the very young love each other and laugh together. The

115

middle generation does the manual work. It's how people were designed to live. You should see Mike reading stories to Margot, doing all the funny voices. It's magic!'

'Don't you all get on top of each other?'

'We meet up when we want to. I've brought you a photo of the front hall – you wouldn't recognise it. It's light and bright with a sofa and a wood-burner. New big windows by the front door, see in this one. We have coffee together there most days – whoever's about. Visitors often call around eleven knowing they'll probably find someone brewing up.'

'What about the garden? My shrubs and bulbs all wrecked by the children no doubt.'

'The garden is the best thing of all. Eddie has taken it over. This year we'll probably be eating most of our own produce. Next year will be even better. He's digging and planting all sorts of stuff. Lots of fruit and nut trees too.'

'It's too shady for fruit surely.'

Noël took a big breath – this could be the tricky bit.

'Eddie has had to take out a few of the pine trees. Not many, but just the ones that kept the best of the sun out. We've got piles of logs stacked in the sheds. They'll last us a couple of winters at least. We need the rest of the pines on the north side as shelter, and to give the house its name of course!'

There was a long silence. Then, grudgingly:

'Well you seem to know what you're doing. I can see the Ladakh connection. You also seem to be happy, even though you haven't yet managed to find yourself a wife.'

This was the other subject that Noël dreaded. It always came up sometime during a visit. His reply surprised him however:

'Well with so many different people coming to the house, friends, and friends of friends, different generations – who knows what might happen.'

His mother smiled a grim smile, but it was tinged with hope. The ordeal was over.

To clinch the argument Noël played the second part of the DVD, 'Paradise With Side-effects' in which two women from Ladakh come to visit England. They wonder at how many things people think they need for a good life, they weep to see old people alone with only a television for company. They go back to Ladakh resolved to preserve some of their own skills and traditions before they are forgotten.

When Stella returned she found Noël and Mother sipping sherry together.

'Chickens I can understand,' Mother was saying, 'but a goat would be going a bit far wouldn't it?'

'Good milk for the twins though,' said Noël, 'and for all of us. Why not? Beth's really keen.'

'Well perhaps I'll come and visit, when it's warmer,' said Mother. Stella raised her eyebrows and looked enquiringly at Noël.

'Have you had a good evening?' she asked.

'Most instructive,' said Mother. 'Your brother has a kind heart, you know.'

33. The First Eleven

Monday had been a Beethoven morning. Mike had started on a boxed set of all nine symphonies.

'Beethoven marked a major turning-point in musical history you know,' he told Noël confidently. Mike's tuition sessions, annoying as they were, signified that he was feeling extremely well.

'That's right, he was' agreed Noël patiently. 'Fancy having coffee a bit early this morning?'

'Why? Don't you appreciate Beethoven? He was one of the…'

'There goes the phone,' said Noël gratefully. 'I'll be back in a minute.'

It was Hilary. She hadn't been able to come for supper the last time they had arranged it as her mother had been taken ill. She had spent several weeks visiting the hospital and then, while Noël was away, her mother had died.

'How's your dad taking it?' asked Noël.

'Working like a maniac,' said Hilary. 'We can't keep up with him in the office. He keeps taking on new projects.'

'Oh Hilary! What a rotten time.' He realised that this was the first time he'd addressed her by name. 'It's funny how names are used,' he thought. 'Sometimes it's to dominate. It's often those who would like to manipulate you that use your name a lot. Yet I don't want to manipulate Hilary, I just want to…'

'Is that supper invitation still valid?' continued Hilary. 'I could do with a change of scene.'

'Of course! Let's see – what about Friday? That's usually a good night for us.'

'That would be great. Thanks.'

Beethoven's Fourth, the one with the manic bassoon solo in the last movement, had just finished. Noël strode towards the CD player and pressed the off button.

'That's a really great work Mike,' he said cheerily. 'Come and have coffee now. Guess what? Hilary's coming to supper on Friday.'

Who's Hilary? Do I know him?'

'She's the architect who did the work here. The big front hall was all her idea. Let's go and have coffee in it.'

'Oh yes. Looks like a boy.'

'That's her.'

Noël looked around the kitchen, as the coffee machine hissed, and sighed. Cleaning the house wasn't one of his favourite things. Everything was beginning to look a bit seedy. Life seemed to be too full of small insistences to do housework, but he didn't want Hilary to think they didn't care for her creation. He didn't mention it to Beth when she came down as he knew she would offer to do it. She had quite enough work with the three children, and it was important to keep the downstairs household independent. After they had finished coffee he phoned Blodwen at the office.

'Hi Blod! I need your advice.'

'Takin' a risk aren't you?' She roared with laughter. Noël moved the phone a couple of inches further away from his ear.

'Do you know of any reliable cleaners, or cleaning agencies around here? You're the nearest person to Ripon, so I thought you might know.'

'I'll put you on to Jean,' she said. 'JEAN!'

'Why Jean?' asked Noël, wincing and rubbing his ear. 'She lives miles away.'

'She had a call from some girls wanting some publicity. They've started a cleaning business in Harrogate. Might be just the thing.'

'Good morning Noël,' came Jean's voice. 'What can I do for you?'

Noël explained.

'The First Eleven' said Jean. 'Peter's going to interview them tomorrow at ten o'clock. Would you like to be present?'

'Sounds like a football team,' said Noël.

'Hockey in fact,' said Jean. 'They were all at Harrogate Ladies' College apparently.'

'Good grief!' said Noël. 'Too posh for us then.'

'That's not my impression. Very practical girls I think. Shall we see you tomorrow?'

'OK. I'll be there.'

The three girls turned up promptly at ten the next morning and sat round the table in the interview room. They were bright-eyed and obviously very excited.

Peter came in and sat facing them, notebook at the ready.

'Now then, how did this project begin?' he asked.

Two of the girls looked at the third, who took a deep breath.

'My name's Emma, and my friends here are Josie and Kath. We were all at Harrogate Ladies' College, as you know. We were all in the First Eleven hockey team and were good friends. After we left we did degrees at different universities, but kept in touch. We've had some holidays together too, so we know that we get on well.' She paused for breath.

Peter nodded, but didn't interrupt. He could sense the bubbling behind her composed manner.

'We all had to have student loans of course, so now we're all technically in debt for a lot of thousands. However you don't have to repay the loan unless you earn above a certain amount. That amount is actually quite possible to live on if you like a simple country life in the north – which we all do.'

Peter nodded. He hadn't written anything so far, and was watching Emma's animated face with a smile on his face. So was Noël.

Emma took a deep breath and continued.

'We're against the growth economy, the way money rules everything people think and do, the way the global corporations are manipulating governments and wrecking the environment…' Here Kath, or Josie, cleared her throat and moved her chair a little.

'Oh sorry! But anyway that's the thinking behind what we want to do. We want to start something simple and then, using our intelligence, help it to grow organically. The simplest thing we could think of was cleaning. Making things beautiful. Cleaning is a dirty word these days, but making someone's home more pleasant to live in is such a great thing to do. On the other hand what we do has got to be fun, and we want to interact with the people we work for.'

At the word 'cleaning' Peter gave a shuddering sigh, but he was still smiling.

'Go on,' he said encouragingly. 'This sounds interesting.'

'The idea is that we work together. A typical day would go like this. We turn up at house number one at nine o'clock. The owner will either be there, or have left breakfast for us. We have breakfast and talk to the owner, or leave a friendly message. We then split up the duties and clean like crazy – all of us. We have music playing if we want to, or else we just open the windows and listen to the birds. An average house should take us an hour. We then go on to house number two. Elevenses there and a similar arrangement. Lunch at house number three. Tea and cake at house number four. This means that we only have one meal to buy and prepare for each working day. This cuts down our living expenses hugely. We share a rented house at the moment and take it in turns to cook. We grow stuff in the garden.'

'That won't give you much of an income to share though will it,' said Peter who had been doing some calculations on his pad.

'Living below the bread-line, but enjoying what we do, is where we start,' said Emma.

'We're going to do some courses,' said Kath, or Josie. 'There are free training courses for all sorts of things available these days. I thought I might do car maintenance. Then we can start offering that too. It will take some time for each of us to be earning a living wage, but we're prepared to look for opportunities and build on them. We'll wait and see what people are actually *wanting* us to do.'

'What about rent? Transport? Council Tax? Insurance?'

'There's help available for people who are working, but earning less than a living wage. While we have to we will accept it, but that isn't how we want to go on. We plan to be a successful co-operative eventually. We've already looked into the legal side of that. Josie's the expert on that sort of thing. Her dad's an accountant.'

At last, by her modest grin, they worked out that the little dark one was Josie.

'We're not going to be sponging off our parents though,' said Josie with a proud flick of her dark fringe. 'We're going to make our own way. There will be the opportunity for exchanges as well as payments. When I've done an accountancy course I can do accounts for other people and they can come and mend our house, or unblock the drains or whatever. We can keep money in its place as a useful tool, but not the only means of exchange. I'm interested in local currencies too… but that's for later.'

'We're starting small, so that we get it right,' said Kath, the one with the fair plait. 'Although our degrees are in subjects that aren't relevant to business, they have taught us to think clearly. Mine's in anthropology!'

Peter closed his notebook and got up.

'Let's see if the photographer is about. He'll probably want you with mops and things – a great cliché man!'

'That's fine,' said Emma. 'When will we be in the paper?'

'Next weekend's Eco-Feature is already booked, but you should be in the week after. I'll get in touch and let you know.'

'Oh yes – don't forget to mention that we don't use chemical cleaning materials. All eco-friendly stuff like soda and vinegar and beeswax and things.'

'Isn't that expensive for you?' asked Peter.

'Oh no! We ask the owners to buy the right materials, otherwise we won't work for them,' grinned Josie. We're asking for organic or local food for our meals too. We're into educating them as well, you see!'

Noël gave a shout of laughter.

'Do you want a job right now?' he asked Emma. My house is in Ripon and has been neglected for months. I've got a visitor coming on Friday who might notice!'

Blodwen came by just as he said this.

'Got a girlfriend then Noël?' she trumpeted. The three girls looked at him expectantly.

'No. It's my architect actually,' he said solemnly. Fortunately Blodwen had sailed on by then. When can you come? What do I need to buy? Which meal should I provide?'

Wednesday was the chosen day, and they agreed to appear at nine o'clock. On the way home Noël called at the organic shop in Ripon and found everything he needed. He decided on organic eggs and bacon, wholemeal bread, cooking apples to make a purée with vanilla and brown sugar, yoghurt. For energy he bought three Fairtrade chocolate bars. This was better than cleaning. It was fun for him too. Musing on past breakfasts he remembered, in Hungary, being given a good slug of brandy. Perhaps that wouldn't do for this occasion. He and Mike could have one though. The excitement of the First Eleven was infectious.

When he got home he rang Peter's home number and left a message: 'Why not ask the First Eleven to do your house too? I'd be happy to give them a meal before they set off, if you're working at the office on Wednesday.'

In the evening he had a text message. 'Already asked them. They're coming after doing you. Been to organic shop so no need for meal. Thanks. P.'

Noël went to find Mike.

'We've got a hockey team coming to clean the house on Wednesday morning. You'll have to get up early and put The Ride of the Valkyries on.'

'I'm not a Wagner man,' said Mike, sternly. 'He's altogether too much.'

'So are these girls,' said Noël. 'You wait!'

Mike and Noël were both in the kitchen when the doorbell rang on Wednesday morning. Noël bounded across the hall and flung the door open.

'Come in. How great to see you all. We're in the kitchen.'

They followed him through and sat round the big table while Noël took orders for how eggs should be done. Their laughter filled the kitchen along with the smell of coffee and freshly toasted bread. Mike had, of course, forgotten who they were, but they explained themselves to him. They had been forewarned about the state of his memory and were careful to be clear, and not to talk too fast. This was quite difficult for Emma, but Noël could see she was thinking carefully about what she said.

'I used to play the violin at school,' said Emma. 'I even got into the orchestra in the end.'

'Nothing like an orchestra,' beamed Mike. 'I spent my whole life in the Hallé you know. They were a great band to work with.'

Kath asked him what instrument he played, and from then on the conversation flowed without interruption.

'Time!' called Emma. 'Let's get on.'

An hour later the house looked immaculate. A faint smell of beeswax floated in the air. The girls had brought flowers for the kitchen table. 'Not imported from Africa or Holland,' insisted Josie. 'Local wild leaves and a few sprigs of winter flowering shrubs from my mum's garden.'

Noël told them just a little about Peter's circumstances, and the fact that he'd been through an extremely difficult time.

'We'd wondered what had been happening. He's actually booked us for double the usual time. He said the house hadn't been touch for many months, and that there had been some nasty spillages and accidents. He's such a neat person himself though.'

'He'll be fine once he's got over the shock of Felicity's death,' said Noël. 'Totally refreshing the house could do the trick.'

'We'll do it!' said Emma. 'If there's spare time we might do a bit to the garden too. We've got time as there are no more bookings today. We won't charge him any more of course – it's our idea, and a way of saying thank you for the publicity.'

'We'll get out of your way then,' said Noël. 'Coming Mike? We'll go down and visit Kay and Jim. They've invited us for coffee.'

'More coffee?' said Mike.

'We could ask for brandy instead.'

'Not a bad idea.'

34. Spring

It had been a wet, cold spring. The young pear tree had bravely produced its blossom but there were no insects to pollinate it. Eddie had tried doing it with a paintbrush but didn't hold out much hope. His spring cabbages were fairly respectable and he'd managed to coax a few salad greens under cloches, but the icy winds had made gardening difficult.

'It's the jet stream,' said Eddie gloomily. 'The arctic ice is melting and is altering its behaviour. It's spending more time over us these days, bringing these bitter winds and gallons of rain.'

Eddie put together the box of vegetables each week for Ivor and Jake. Noël had tried insisting on paying for the bought items, but Eddie wouldn't hear of it.

'You've changed our lives,' he said with a grin. 'My contribution is topping up the veg box. It will spur me on to growing more.'

'The weather is working against you, and that's not fair,' said Noël.

'Weather is something we have to live with,' said Eddie, 'particularly if it's our fault that the climate's changing. I'm going to make a growing-house for next winter – part solid, part glass. We can keep the hens in there to keep it warm.'

'When shall we get hens?' asked Noël.

'Just as soon as I've done some more fencing. They are going to have several grassy spaces so we can rotate them around. Keep them off the vegetable beds. Margot can't wait, so I'd better get on with it, rain or no rain.' He put his empty mug down and went across the hall to where his muddy boots stood on newspapers. He hunched his waterproofs over his shoulders and opened the front door. A gust of wind flung the newspapers across the hall. As Noël gathered them up he wondered whether a porch on the front-door would be a good idea.

'Must ask Hilary about that.'

Mike appeared from his room and tapped across to the sofa.

'Are we going out today?' he asked.

'I've got to go and do some work,' said Noël. 'Isn't Gerald coming?'

'Who?'

'Gerald – you know. That nice chap who does photography and takes you out sometimes.'

'Don't remember any of that.'

'I'll just check the diary, but I'm sure it's today. The weather's a bit rough though.'

'Is it?'

'Just take a look!'

Mike went to the front door and opened it. The wind swung the door back catching Mike on the shoulder. He staggered and fell. Noël rushed forward to help him up. Fortunately he didn't hit his head this time, but he was shaken.

'Here, come and sit on the sofa. Take it easy for a bit.'

'I don't want to go out there,' said Mike, fearfully.

'Don't blame you,' said Noël. 'Shall I give Gerald a ring and put it off?'

'Who's Gerald?'

'That chap who takes you out sometimes when I'm working.'

'Do you *have* to go out to work?'

'I've got a couple of pieces to do for the paper. They have to be in before tomorrow.'

'Can't you write them here?'

Noël thought carefully.

'I've left the books down at the office in town,' he said carefully, hating himself. They were in his writing-bag of course. He hated lying to Mike and knew he would curse himself for the rest of the day. Mike deserved the truth like anybody else. What's more Noël didn't feel like leaving him now.

'I'll just get you a glass of water,' he said, playing for time, and went into the kitchen. He dialled Gerald's number.

'Mike's just had a bit of a fall, and the weather's terrible. What do you think about today?'

'I was thinking of bringing a slide-show over,' said Gerald. 'Some of the images I took last summer, what there was of it!'

'Perfect!' said Noël. 'I'll stay here until you come and then go off and work for a bit.' He filled a glass and went back to Mike in the hall. 'Glass of water. Gerald's coming after lunch, but you're not going out today. It's just too horrible.'

'Who?'

'The photographer chap. Used to be a geography teacher.'

'Oh him. You mean *Gerald*?'

'Yes, that's right. Gerald.'

Noël breathed deeply and deliberately to slow his heart rate. He would go and find something quiet to do until lunchtime, and do his writing this afternoon. Where was that recipe for spring cabbage that Beth had given him? Something about shredding the cabbage and mixing it with noodles. He would make a copy of it for Ivor and put it into the next veg box.

The afternoon's writing went well. Noël found that, given a calm and peaceful corner, words still came easily.

'God knows what would happen if that stopped,' he thought. There had been several periods in his life when the flow had seized up, and he had worried that the stresses of looking after Mike might create so much tension in his brain that it ceased to operate. As the time approached for each 'respite week' he could feel this starting to happen. Three-monthly intervals seemed to be just about right to keep in balance. He still felt guilty about it though.

'Mike, I'm home,' he called as he wrestled with the front door against the wind. 'Come and have some tea in the kitchen. I called at Calthwaite's for some tea-cakes.'

Mike came through looking extremely pleased with himself, and walked with more confidence than usual.

'That chap Gerald's just gone,' he said. 'He showed me some wonderful pictures that he'd strung together in a, in a... in a sort of film show. We talked about putting music with it, and I was able to give him a bit of advice. I suggested a sequence of English music – Vaughan Williams, Delius, Butterworth – d'you know he hadn't heard 'The Banks of Green Willow' before?'

'What a wonderful idea,' said Noël. 'You were always a bit of an English music champion. Do you remember that long conversation we had once about what makes English music sound English? I don't think we ever reached a conclusion. Something to do with the landscape, and a certain feeling of longing, or regret maybe – but not unhappiness.'

'I lent him some of my CDs and he's coming again in a couple of weeks to show me what he's done.'

'Brilliant!'

'Now then,' said Mike purposefully, 'I've been thinking about dying.'

Noël dropped the teaspoons. 'Umm... not today I hope – there are teacakes to be eaten!' Noël slid them under the grill and got the butter dish out. He held his breath for Mike's next words.

'No. When we played some Gurney songs today, and I thought about death, and about Mary in that place in ....' Mike stopped.

'Only her remains are there,' said Noël quietly. 'Mary lives on in the beautiful things she made, and in our memories.'

'Alone in that Place,' repeated Mike fiercely. 'That icy-cold priest who called her 'our dear departed brother' by mistake, and then wanted to shake my hand at the end. "Get it right next time" I shouted at him. But there won't be a next time..... not for Mary.'

Noël wished he had been there, and watched Mike helplessly as he struggled with his memories and his anger.

'I want to stay here,' continued Mike firmly. 'I want to be buried under the pine trees and give something back to the garden when my time comes. I want to stay in the place that I love.'

'Now there's a thought!' said Noël. 'There's quite a lot of 'green burial' going on these days. People hate formal funerals because they are such Big Business these days. They want something more personal and loving. I'll see what I can find out. Not sure that you can be dug into your own garden though.'

'And you can play the Butterworth,' continued Mike. 'I'm sure some of the Hallé gang would come and play it for me.'

'Well, Sir George Howard had the LSO trombones playing Beethoven *Equali* at his funeral at Castle Howard,' said Noël, remembering the article he'd written about it for the Musical Times. 'I think they really enjoyed the outing!'

'You'd give them a good tea wouldn't you?' said Mike, tucking in to his teacake, butter dripping down his shirt. 'Musicians will do anything if there's a good meal afterwards!'

'What makes you think I'll still be here,' laughed Noël. 'I might go first.'

Mike wasn't listening, but had started humming the Butterworth.

*

'First day of bloody sunshine this year and you start talking about Death!' shouted Blodwen the next morning. 'What's got into you Noël?'

'It's Mike,' said Noël.

'Oh I'm sorry…' Blodwen came down a decibel or two. 'What's happened?'

'It's OK. He's fine – in particularly good form as a matter of fact. He was just thinking about not being slotted away in a municipal cemetery. His wife was buried at that awful place in Ardwick. She had a hideously impersonal service too. He wants to be buried at Treetops.'

'Jesus! That'll knock some value off your property!'

'Not my main concern, Blod. It's not going to be sold – it belongs to a Trust.' Anyway people are buried all over the place. They're only made of carbon, nitrogen and water you know. Quite decent stuff really. Good for the crops.'

'Well don't come offering me your flamin' *surplus carrots*!' roared Blodwen as she executed a dramatic exit. Noël wondered how she managed to make everything sound like a *double entendre* and mused on alternative meanings for 'surplus carrots.'

Peter came in at that moment and raised his eyebrows.

'What *have* you been offering Blodwen?'

'Oh it's OK. We were talking gardening, and green burial too.'

'Who's being buried?'

'Mike wanted to know if he could be buried at Treetops, that's all.'

'I did a piece about a local green burial site a couple of months ago,' said Peter. 'There's a book somewhere. Perhaps you ought to review it for the paper.'

'Can you remember what it's called?'

'Something about Natural Death I think,' said Peter.

'I thought all death was fairly natural,' said Noël. 'Not many alternatives are there?'

'You'd think there was the way some of the media treat it,' said Peter sighing.

'Sorry Peter. Didn't mean to treat it lightly.'

'It's OK. I'm beginning to get over Felicity's suicide now.'

'Was it definitely suicide then?'

'Yes. It seems she'd been watching the staff, and the other patients, extremely carefully and managing to get hold of various pills. When she'd got a good number together she took the whole lot. Her liver couldn't cope. Nobody suspected, and they're still not sure how she managed it. Security is very tight there. There's been a huge investigation, but no one person is to blame it seems.'

'You wouldn't think that was possible,' said Noël. 'Those places are always tremendously careful with drugs.'

'Well she did it,' said Peter, shrugging. 'She had a death-wish even when I first met her as a student. It was only a matter of time. Such a brilliant brain though. Such a waste.'

'How did The First Eleven get on?' asked Noël to change the subject. Peter's face lit up.

'They were wonderful. When I got home the house smelled of fresh air and beeswax. There were flowers on the kitchen table and in the sitting-room. They had even cleared the overhanging stuff each side of the garden path.'

'Good. They did a great job for us too. I'm going to ask them to come every three weeks, just to keep us in good order.'

'So am I,' laughed Peter. 'I don't make much mess, living on my own, so that should be often enough. They left a message asking whether I'd like them to go on doing the garden too.'

'Can they make a living at it do you think?'

'Well they've got the determination. I don't think they even consider failure.'

Noël settled at a desk and switched on his laptop. He searched 'Natural Death' and found what he wanted: The Natural Death Centre. They had just published a new edition of their handbook. Resisting the temptation to order it from an Internet Giant he made a note of the details and emailed The Little Ripon Bookshop. Ripon still managed to support an independent bookshop, and enlightened locals were determined that it should survive.

35. Summer

'Phew!' said Noël as he entered the office.

'You sound like the bloody Daily Mirror!' hollered Blodwen. 'What's the matter with you?'

'We've had so much cold, I can't cope with this heat.'

'Go on! It's grand. Are you havin' a holiday this summer? How's Mike?'

'Mike's fine, but – well – getting older.'

'Aren't we all, except you of course!'

'Am I keeping it hidden then?'

'Yeah! You're not bad for your age. Ha!' Blodwen gave him a playful shove, and he staggered against the wall.

Jean looked up with a prim smile and slid a pile of books towards him.

'Mostly financial this time I'm afraid.'

'Shouldn't Peter have those?'

'The Chief doesn't want specialist pieces, but something more general. The human side of the financial crisis, and how it happened. There's a DVD here too somewhere – I took it home and it's good. It tells you where money actually comes from.' Jean rummaged in her bag. 'Here it is. 'Positive Money' by Ben Dyson. He seems an intelligent young man and has done his research thoroughly. He gives hundreds of talks all over the country. He was on Radio 4 last week.'

'I'll start with that then,' said Noël, and packed the books into his bag. The DVD went into his pocket. As he drove back to Ripon he thought about his mornings at Ivor and Jake's house. Perhaps he could stop going there and do his work at home after Mike had gone to bed. Then he could spend more time with him during the day. Mike was increasingly uneasy when Noël went out.

'No. That's not the answer,' piped up his inner voice.

'Haven't heard from you for a while,' said Noël.

'That's because you haven't been doing anything stupid!'

'Ah.'

'If you work at night, it would have to be several nights each week. You would be extremely tired during the day. You know how difficult it is to deal with Mike's anxieties and repetitions when you're tired. That's when you snap.'

'True. So what's the answer then, Oh Clever One?'

'The First Eleven?'

'But we don't need more cleaning.'

'Didn't they say that they were thinking of doing other things too? Things that people actually *wanted* them to do?'

'Oh yes. So they did.'

'Ring Emma.'

'OK Boss.'

It was still stiflingly hot when Emma came to Treetops the following week. Ivor and Jake had been the day before and Ivor had made iced coffee for them all.

'Special recipe I picked up at work,' said Ivor. 'It's got cardamom and cream in it. Jake loves it. Oh by the way, Jake has an idea to tell you about.'

Jake's blue eyes were wide and sparkling. He waved his arms about the spacious hall where they were sitting, and then pointed at the wood-burner.

'Nice hot stove!'

'Surely you don't want the stove to be lit? We'd die of heat-stroke!'

'I want to make a coloured one. One just for you!' Jake beamed at Noël and reached out to touch his hand.

'It's the rugs they make at the Quaker workshop,' explained Ivor. 'Jake wants to make a special one for the hall here. He loves this place so much.'

'That would be wonderful,' said Noël. 'What a great idea. Shall we take some measurements?'

'Round one,' beamed Jake. 'Big round one. I like rounds – they make me happy.'

'To go with the stove it would have to have a hole in the middle and go all round it,' said Noël. 'Is that what you want to do? It would take ages to make.'

'Yes!' shouted Jake and jumped up. 'All round it with lots of colours.'

How Mother would hate it, thought Noël, grinning. He turned to Jake and squeezed his hand. 'It'll be grand. I can't wait to see it!'

The next day Noël told Emma about the rug as they sipped their iced coffee, and then told her a bit about Ivor and Jake. She looked thoughtful.

'Is this chap Ivor happy working at the supermarket?'

'Well he's one of those people who can find the good in anything I think,' said Noël. 'He says he's learning a lot about humanity. He did a degree in sociology, and finds his job feeds into that remarkably well! He's not earning much though.'

'We're looking around for another pair of hands for The First Eleven,' continued Emma. 'We can't afford to pay anyone yet, but we're keeping our eyes open. He sounds our sort of person.'

'Yes he's your sort of person alright,' said Noël. 'He's always positive, and extremely bright.'

'Thank you for the compliment!' Emma smiled mischievously. 'Perhaps we can arrange to meet up with him for a drink sometime. Josie's very good at assessing character. I tend to get over-enthusiastic too soon.'

As Mike was out they were able to talk about him at some length. He was spending the morning with Gerald.

'I couldn't expect you to cover for me *every* working morning,' he said. 'Mike doesn't really need constant attention, he just likes it!'

'We share an interest in music,' said Emma thoughtfully. 'At school I loved playing the violin but never did any history of music.'

'That's Mike's Great Thing,' laughed Noël. 'He's always giving me improving lectures on musical matters.'

'Well, how about this,' said Emma, thinking carefully as she spoke. 'I hate the idea of being a 'carer'. It implies something patronising – I can't quite put my finger on it, but I don't like it. That doesn't mean I don't want to care, but if someone is identified as a carer it implies that other people don't care. It also turns being kind to someone into a paid job.'

'Oh how true!' said Noël. 'Just once, when I was checking in to a holiday cottage I used that awful word. The owner asked if I was planning a walking holiday. To my shame I answered that I was a full-time carer, and just needed a rest. That woman's face melted into pity and condolence, and I felt deeply ashamed.'

'But you do care for Mike full-time. Even if you're not here you're organising for him, and thinking about him.'

'Yes, but her pity was misplaced. Being with Mike is fun. We get on well and have lots of laughs. He appreciates my cooking. The fact that some of his mental faculties are a bit wobbly is incidental. I just have to be on form to cope with them that's all. My position isn't caring so much as – well – sharing I suppose. That sounds horribly pious, sorry, but I've chosen to share my life with him, and that's what I'm doing. Trying to do it intelligently, that's all…'

'How about a weekly music lesson?' said Emma, after a pause. 'I would enjoy that, and I think Mike would too. He would be using his knowledge and experience, rather than being just 'minded'. He would have to do some preparation too, which would give him something constructive to do when you're not here.'

'That's an inspired idea,' said Noël. 'I'll ask Mike what he thinks about it this afternoon and give you a ring. We can take it from there.'

When Mike came in at lunchtime he was exhausted.

'We went to Brimham Rocks again,' he said. 'Gerald wanted to add to his 'funny shapes in nature' collection but it was too hot. I just sat on a – thing – wooden thing – under a tree, you know. Even then it was too hot.'

'I'll make you an iced coffee,' said Noël. 'It's Ivor's recipe and very good.'

When he carried it through Mike had fallen asleep on his bed with his shoes on. Noël crept out and drank the coffee himself. He was barely able to suppress his excitement about Emma's idea, but realised Mike would need to feel more alert before he could tackle it.

It was another two days before Noël had found the right moment to ask Mike about the music lessons. The idea was so good that he was afraid of getting it wrong. He needn't have worried.

'Hi Emma! It's Noël. Mike is delighted about the music lessons. He's already getting books and files out, and making notes.'

'That's wonderful,' said Emma. 'I've even played my violin a bit since I saw you. It sounded terrible, but that's not the point! It's music history that interests me now.'

'He used to teach oboe part-time at a specialist music school in Manchester,' said Noël. 'He loved the atmosphere there and would have liked to do more I know.'

'So he's not anxious about it then?'

'Not at all. The interesting thing is that, although he forgets words a lot these days – quite ordinary nouns mostly – his music vocabulary is absolutely intact. I suppose it's well fixed in his long-term memory. He gave me a long lecture last night about a teaching method he'd devised, but never tried. He's got all his research notes somewhere.'

'Help! What's that?'

'Something about not starting with cave-men and bones, and working forward to Stockhausen, but doing the whole thing in reverse. It's to do with finding links, the small things that tie each era of music to the previous one. He said that if children learned what today's composers were doing, and understood it better, then contemporary music would have a bigger audience.'

'Right! I'd better get my brain dusted off,' laughed Emma. 'When shall we begin?'

'Well we're planning a short trip to Scotland next week,' said Noël. 'Somewhere cooler I hope. Shall we start at the beginning of September, like a school term?'

'That's fine,' said Emma. 'We can fix which days I come when you get back. By the way we're meeting Ivor this evening down at The Water Rat. He sounds quite keen.'

'That's good,' said Noël. 'I hope it works out.'

'We've devised a puzzle for him,' laughed Emma. 'We're trying to find a good word for the people we work for. We don't like 'customers' or 'clients' – or even 'victims'!'

'Poor Ivor! I hope he survives.'

'We'll be kind to him - that's what we do after all.'

The trip to Scotland was a welcome change, but not exactly relaxing for Noël. They drove to Ardrossan, taking a couple of days over it, and then took the ferry to Arran. They had booked a room in a hotel overlooking the harbour, and Mike spent most of the mornings sitting by the window watching the activities in the bay. He often dropped off to sleep in the armchair, and then woke with a start wondering fearfully where he was. This meant that Noël's mornings had to be spent in the room with him. After lunch they went for a drive and explored the island, but as Mike couldn't walk far the delights of the glens and beaches, and the enticing path up Goat Fell were not possible. By teatime Mike was exhausted and had to return to their room for a nap before dinner. By the end of the four days Noël's frustration had exhausted him too, and he found himself dozing fitfully during the day, in between reading the limited range of books available in the hotel, and unable to sleep at night. Getting home to Ripon was a relief.

36. Autumn

'Can I speak to Hilary please?'

'Just a moment. I'll put you through.'

The metallic strains of Vivaldi's 'Four Seasons' invaded Noël's ear. He moved the phone away and gritted his teeth. Why do they all choose that?

'Hilary Forsyth speaking.'

'It's Noël, trying again! How many times have you *not* been to supper with us now?'

'Oh Noël! How good of you to ring. I think it's probably three times altogether. I do feel bad about it.'

'How's your father now?'

'Recovering well. It was only a mild stroke. His speech is very slightly slurred, but you'd have to know him well to notice it. He gets tired easily though.'

'Are you having to look after him all the time? Could I tempt you to make another supper date?'

'Yes please. I'd love that. There's a bit of a plan afoot at the family home which I'll tell you about. It will mean that I'm much less tied down.'

'Good. What about next Friday?'

'Oh dear, you've said that before so many times. Do you think Friday is bad luck or something?'

'OK let's make it Saturday night – a much more festive night. Then you can lie in on Sunday morning.'

'Fine. It's in the diary.'

As he put the phone down he heard laughter from the kitchen. Emma was just finishing breakfast. Mike had got up in a hurry, buttoned his shirt up all wrong, and gone through to join her. As Noël went in Emma was undoing the shirt so that he could start again.

'Hi Noley! I'm just being undressed by this girl...'

'That's Emma, who's come for her music lesson.'

'I know that. I'm not daft – just stupid that's all.'

'Don't worry about it,' said Emma. 'There. You're decent now.'

'Unusual for a young girl like you to want to know about music,' said Mike. 'Most of them seem hooked on pop these days.'

'Isn't pop music 'music' then?' asked Emma.

'It's something else,' said Mike firmly. 'It's something that took off in the fifties and sixties, driven by fear.'

Noël's eyebrows went up. He moved quietly away to sit at the far end of the kitchen. This was a theory he hadn't heard before, and he wanted to listen in.

'Fear?' said Emma. 'What of?'

'That generation had seen what an atom bomb could do. They felt the world was finished. It was only a matter of time before we wiped ourselves out. They buried themselves in the sort of compelling sound that stopped them thinking about it.'

'Go on,' said Emma, pushing her chair back and crossing her legs.

'It had a constant beat that gave them comfort. It recreated the steady beat of the mother's heart that you hear in the womb. And if it's loud it represents that other insistent beat of life… er… um… not sure how to put it…'

'Fucking?' said Emma helpfully.

'Er, yes. Oops! Sorry about that!'

'I see...'

'Then big business and drug dealers got in on the act and it took over the lives, and the pocket-money, of the whole generation. It's worse nowadays because they plug the stuff straight into their brains with those… those things in their ears.'

'Headphones?'

'Yes, headphones. Now the music I spent my life playing, is an art form. It's meant to engage and enrich the brain, not to hypnotise or deaden it. I thought we'd start your first lesson with something simple.'

'Oh good,' said Emma with relief. 'What's it to be?'

'The Unanswered Question,' said Mike. 'Let's go through to the other room and I'll play it to you.'

At this point Noël slid softly towards the door. Outside in the hall he wiped his forehead, picked up his bag and set off, somewhat distractedly, to do his morning's work.

Later that evening Emma rang.

'That lesson was quite something!' she said, laughing. 'Music will never sound quite the same again.'

'I didn't realise he was that good,' said Noël. 'I get so offended when he tries to tell me simple facts about music that

I've usually found a reason to get him to stop. I feel ashamed of myself.'

'He's given me homework too. I've got to find out all about someone called Steve Reich.'

'Oh yes,' said Noël. 'That should be fun. By the way, how did the meeting with Ivor go?'

'I do love Ripon,' said Emma. 'On the day that our Prime Minister was taking a vote on whether to start a war in the Middle East the local newspaper was delightfully oblivious!'

'Why? What was the headline?'

'I just happened to see it on the pub piano. It said "Who shot Teddy the Cat?"'

'Nice!' said Noël. 'It's good to keep a balance in these things.'

'Oh, and I met The Wakeman too. He was in for a pint before doing his thing in the market place. He gave me a lucky wooden penny.'

'George is quite a character isn't he?' said Noël. 'It's amazing that there's been a Wakeman blowing his horn every night in Ripon for more than a thousand years.'

'It certainly is. I asked him what note he was playing. He reckoned it was Db, unless the weather was extreme, which changed the length of his horn slightly.'

'I can see your lesson with Mike has made you more musically aware! Did you get on well with Ivor?'

'Oh yes, he's just the sort of chap we'd like to join our team. He had some really good ideas.'

'Did he answer your question about what to call your customers?'

'Yes. He suggested we called them people.'

'Calling people 'people' seems eminently sensible to me.'

'Us too. He's going to do another six months at the supermarket and then see where we've got to.'

'So you'll be going on with Mike's lessons then?'

'Yes, the next one's already booked. It's great being paid to learn!'

'The government used to do something like that in the past. I had a grant to study music in London. We were the lucky generation. They seem to have got their values in a twist these days – too much influence from the business world.'

'The best idea seems to be to forget about the government and just get on and do stuff.'

'That sounds like anarchist talk!'

'Well perhaps I am one then. Not a bomb-throwing one, just trying to make life good in my own way.'

'That'll do very well,' said Noël. 'Join the Benign Anarchists' Society!'

He put the phone down still grinning to himself. Now wouldn't it be good if Ivor and Emma… no, don't even think of interfering. Anyway perhaps Emma…

'Excuse me,' said his inner voice.

'What do you want?'

'Remember your age. It's time to go to bed and get some rest ready for tomorrow. You've got to take Mike to the dentist.'

Noël sighed, turned out the light and made his way towards his room. Moonlight was flooding into the hall. He stopped to feel the last of the warmth from the wood-burner on his back and looked out at the trees waving gently against a marbled sky. Yes life was good, very good. Even so this didn't stop him tossing and turning thinking about the next day. Going to the dentist meant a drive to Manchester as Mike hadn't been able to find a local dentist who could take him on. It meant difficult parking. It meant reminding Mike several times why they were going there. In his dreams he went round and round the city, but found every parking place full. In the end he parked his car, which had somehow turned into a boat, on the Bridgewater Canal. But that was nowhere near the dentist's so they had to get a taxi. There were no taxis, apart from a shabby black car with an orange rug on the back seat. The driver didn't know the street where the dentist's was. If they missed the appointment Mike would be struck off the list and then wouldn't have a dentist at all. Noël woke at five o'clock sweating, and went into the kitchen for a cup of tea.

He managed a couple more hours sleep after that, but they were not pleasant. He dreamt that Emma was telling him about her financial adviser's experience with a meat processing company. The company manager was looking for funding for a new machine. It looked like a huge box with a hopper on top and a tube coming out of the bottom. Whole pigs, heads feet and all, were dropped into the hopper, the machine ground and shuddered and a pink paste oozed out of the bottom. 'I'll never be eating their sausages again,' said the financial adviser. Noël woke shaking. The trouble was that this dream was true, just as Emma had told him.

'No more bacon for me at breakfast please,' she had said the previous week. 'I'm going completely vegetarian from now on.'

'What sparked that?' Noël had asked.

'A story our financial adviser told me,' said Emma. 'It was the last straw.'

*

'Can you give me a hand?' called Eddie. He was standing at the front door with a wheel-barrow. A large basket of logs was balanced on the top, wobbling slightly. Noël took one handle and Eddie, kicking off his boots, took the other. They carried the basket over to the wood-burner in the hall.

'What on earth is that?' asked Eddie.

'That's the first segment of Jake's rug,' said Noël. 'He's making one to go around the stove. The workshop suggested doing it in sections, like an orange. He liked that idea. I just put it there to see if the size is right.'

'It's going to be like a sea of flame if he goes on like that,' said Eddie. 'But it will take him years to finish.'

'I think some of the others are helping him,' said Noël. 'He's so enthusiastic that they all want to join in.'

'Do you want to light the stove now?'

'Yes, I want to get it going early today. Hilary's coming to supper.'

'At last!' said Eddie. 'I hope nothing goes wrong this time.'

'I'm going to ask her about putting a porch on the front of the house. Not big enough to block those amazing windows, but somewhere for boots and things.'

'Good idea,' said Eddie. 'We could keep a back-up store of logs there too in another basket.'

'It would have to be a narrow one, but it would be useful if we ran out on a mucky night.'

'Beth is thinking about the twins' first birthday later this month. Margot will be three soon after so we might have a combined party. We hope you'll both come.'

'Would you like it down here?' asked Noël. 'They could have tea in the kitchen and tear around in here afterwards.'

141

'I'll see what Beth thinks. That's a kind and brave offer.'

'Mike loves having the children around. He'll probably read them a story if they get too rowdy.'

Noël went back to the kitchen where the results of his recent shopping trip were scattered all over the big table. Beth had given him a recipe for Spanakopitta using spinach, onions and cheese. He put on his striped apron and tried to feel confident.

Suddenly there was a crash, and a loud yell. He dropped the onions and ran into the hall. Silence. He burst into Mike's room and found him surrounded by CDs and looking extremely upset.

'Noley,' he wailed, 'I've pulled the whole damn lot down.' The shelf had toppled forward, fortunately missing Mike's head, and his entire CD collection had slid on to the floor. Noël's heart was racing and he felt sick. He sat down on the bed and looked helplessly at the mess. Beth appeared at the door looking anxious.

'What on earth was that?' she asked.

'Just an avalanche,' said Noël through gritted teeth. He couldn't help remembering the fate of the French composer Alkan, and his heart was racing.

'I'll give you a hand in a minute,' said Beth. I'll just go and check on the twins. Eddie must fix the shelf to the wall so it can't happen again.'

'I can't think how it wasn't fixed in the first place,' said Noël.

'I think we weren't sure where it was going,' said Mike. I didn't know if I wanted the CDs by my chair or near the… the thing… the thing that plays them '

'Well do you know now, for heavens' sake?' shouted Noël. His fear had made him furious, like a mother whose child has run into the road.

'It'll be fine where it is,' said Mike. 'Or rather not where it is now, but where it was… before…'

Noël stormed off into the kitchen. He reached for the whisky bottle and poured himself a couple of fingers. His hand was shaking.

'Pull yourself together, and only drink half that,' said his inner voice sternly. 'Mike's fine.'

'Today of all days,' grumbled Noël. He snatched the apron off and threw it on the table. Crossing the hall he opened the front door, strode over to the bench and sat down with his whisky glass. A few leaves, red, cream and golden, were rolling gently across the grass. The pine trees sighed. Eddie, in the far corner, was lifting the last of the potatoes which lay shining on the dark soil.

'Hmm!' said his inner voice. 'Better now? How lucky are you?'

Eddie looked up and waved a muddy hand.

'This row is great. Lots of big baking-size ones. All the rows have been different for some reason. Taking a break from the kitchen?'

'Mike's just crashed his CD shelf down on the floor,' said Noël. 'Gave me the fright of my life. I've come out to recover.'

'Didn't we fix it to the wall?' said Eddie puzzled. 'Oh no, I remember now. He wasn't sure where he wanted it. Is he hurt?'

'No, thank God.'

'I'll fix it straight after lunch. I'm really sorry, I should have checked.'

Noël tipped the last of the whisky on a dandelion and got up.

'Back to the kitchen sink for me then,' he said, smiling. 'Beth said she'd help Mike sort the mess out.'

*

Noël opened the front door and suddenly felt dreadfully awkward. He hadn't seen Hilary for months, and now realised that he hardly knew her. They had been very easy on the phone, but he'd forgotten the bounce of her hair, her ready smile, her boyish figure. She was wearing a canvas cap with a peak, rather like the first time she had come. She took it off as he opened the door. Her navy shirt and jeans were topped off with a multi-coloured waistcoat of wine reds and rich greens with a touch of gold thread. Her….

'Can I come in?' grinned Hilary.

Noël pulled his brain into focus and stepped back, embarrassed.

'It's lovely to see you,' he said, opening the door wide. 'Sorry, I'd sort of forgotten what you looked like!'

'It's been an awful long time,' said Hilary, stepping in and looking around. 'Wow! you've made this into a wonderful space.'

'You made the space,' said Noël. 'We've just been putting things in it.'

'I mean the whole atmosphere. It gives such a warm welcome.'

'We love it too,' said Noël, 'and so do all our friends. We get lots of visitors, particularly at coffee time in the mornings. Come and sit on the sofa and I'll get you a drink. What would you like?'

Mike emerged from his room and tapped across to sit beside Hilary. He leaned over and gave her a hug. Noël blinked. Why hadn't he thought of that?

'Good to see you again,' said Mike. 'Forgotten your name though.'

'Hilary,' said Noël and Hilary both together, then laughed. 'It was Hilary who redesigned the house for us,' said Noël. 'Remember?'

'No I don't remember, but I remember her nice face,' said Mike, smiling happily. 'What's for supper?'

The evening went with a swing after that. They disposed of a couple of bottles of wine, the Spanakopitta was a success, and the peaches in brandy with whipped cream made an elegant finish. Mike yawned and smiled appreciatively.

'Great cooking Noley. I think I'll have to go to bed now though, I'm knackered.'

'I'll come and help you with your socks and shoes,' said Noël. Mike had been finding them increasingly difficult to deal with. It reminded Noël of John Mortimer's autobiography where he said something like "The day I knew I was *really* old was when I found I couldn't put my socks on." For this reason he usually held back from helping Mike. He didn't want him to feel really old before he needed to. Maybe it was the wine, but tonight he wanted, for some reason, to be particularly kind. Or perhaps he needed to leave the room for a moment, because from now on he would be alone with Hilary...

'You're so good with Mike,' said Hilary when he got back.

'Not always I'm afraid,' said Noël, sitting down opposite her and filling her glass, and then his own. 'I get pretty tight-lipped sometimes, and have been known to lose it altogether.'

'But that's normal,' said Hilary. 'Doesn't everybody? You should hear me with my Dad sometimes!'

'Don't you find both living and working with him a strain?' asked Noël.

'Oh I don't *live* with him,' laughed Hilary. 'That would be a disaster. I've spent quite a time there recently of course, but I've got my own place and have had for years.'

'Where's that?' asked Noël.

'It's one of those new houses down by the canal basin,' said Hilary. 'One of our team designed them and I bought the first one when they were finished. It's a great place to live. Away from the centre of town, calm water in front, but just a short walk from the market place. Particularly if you cut through by The Water Rat, over the river and up behind the cathedral.'

'Oh I know it so well!' said Noël wistfully. 'I lived on the canal for years. Do you remember a boat called Archimedes?'

'Oh was that you?' said Hilary. 'Yes, I remember it. It's still there, down beyond the lock isn't it?'

'That's right. There's an artist living in it now, but he's away a lot. I miss being on the water, but it made sense to come up here when I inherited the house. I was getting a bit old for life on a narrow boat.'

'Rubbish!' said Hilary. 'I bet you'd love to be back there really. I can tell from the way you talk about it.'

'Yes I've a feeling you're right,' said Noël, 'but Mike couldn't manage it – no way.'

Hilary looked thoughtful. There were several things she wanted to say about that, but felt it best to keep them to herself for the time being.

'Nightcap?' asked Noël.

'Yes, if you'll get me a taxi afterwards,' said Hilary. 'Can we go back into the hall, by the stove?'

They settled on the sofa. Noël got up and turned off the overhead light. The two lamps each side of the sofa made it feel intimate, making him nervous again. He went to the stove and poked the logs about, pushing another one in to the blazing flames.

'Dad's going to be looked after really well soon,' said Hilary. 'There's a couple coming to live in. The wife will do the house-keeping and her husband will look after the garden and the maintenance. They've just come over from Romania and are tremendous fun. Their English is quirky, but pretty good, and they love my Dad.'

'How did you get to know them?' asked Noël. There were so many negative stories around about immigrants that it was good to hear a positive one.

'Their daughter Rosa studied architecture in Bucharest,' said Hilary. 'She did a year's exchange with a chap from our office. She stayed with my parents, and later they had a holiday in Romania and visited her family. When Mum died Emil and Dora offered to come over and help Dad. Then he had the stroke and they decided to stay permanently. Getting visas was a nightmare, but eventually it all worked out and they're coming at the end of the month.'

'What a relief for you,' said Noël.

'Oh yes,' said Hilary, laughing. 'We'd have killed each other if I'd had to go on looking after him. He's hoping to get back to work by the beginning of next year, so they will have a fairly easy time, at least to begin with. It's such a relief to know they'll be there if he's ill again.'

The conversation flowed easily after that. They talked about their various travels and Hilary soon realised how much Noël missed his freedom, although he insisted that his life at Treetops was absolutely fine. It was well after midnight when Hilary suddenly jumped up.

'I really must go. Can I use your phone to get a taxi? I 'accidentally' left my mobile behind in case Dad tried to get in touch.'

'It's in the kitchen,' said Noël. 'Help yourself.' He settled back comfortably on the sofa and felt more relaxed than he could remember. He wondered how soon he could invite her again.

'Taxi in ten minutes,' said Hilary. 'I'm lucky, as it's Saturday night. The town will be full of drunks like me wanting to get home.'

'Will you come back for your car in the morning?' asked Noël.

'I came up on the bus, thinking I'd walk home,' said Hilary. 'There's a full moon tonight, but I don't honestly think I could make it. Too much hospitality!'

Noël felt disappointed, although meeting on the 'morning after' anything was usually rather a bleak affair. They heard a scrunch on the gravel outside. Noël went to open the front door and Hilary pulled her cap from her pocket and stuck it crookedly on her head. They stood opposite each other in the doorway. Noël put out his hand and then suddenly snatched it back.

'Wait! I nearly forgot. We were going to ask you about putting a porch on the front door. The weather crashes in here sometimes. Do you think it could be done without taking too much light from the windows?'

Hilary looked up at him and grinned mischievously.

'I think that calls for a professional visit. Would you mind ringing the office to make an appointment?'

She then reached up and put her warm hands on each side of his face. She kissed him lightly on the nose and the peak of her cap tickled his hair.

'Thanks for a lovely evening. Say goodbye to Mike for me. He's a lucky bloke.'

As the tail-lights eased away between the bushes Noël looked up at the full moon, and stayed looking at it for a long time.

37. Winter

October was a glorious month. The long cold spring and the late hot summer had brought out some startling autumn colours, and a few of them still decorated the trees. Noël liked this time of year, especially after the clocks went back. It reminded him of winter evenings on the boat. He used to draw the curtains, light the tiny gas stove, pour a glass of wine and plump up the cushions in his armchair ready for a good long read. When he was working full time this was a rare treat. He was so often out at concerts and then had to write up before going to bed. These days he was pleased not to be going out so often.

He rang Hilary's office and arranged an appointment for the next Friday afternoon. He had waited about a fortnight before ringing. He didn't want to sound too eager. The memory of their evening together gave him a warm feeling whenever he thought about it. Hilary had sent him a CrazyDog e-card as a thank-you, and he'd opened it several times since. The dog idea was something else they had forgotten to talk about.

Friday morning, when he took Mike's breakfast tray in he was surprised to hear the unctuous tones of 'The World's *Grrreatest* Music. *This* is Clllassic FM'. Mike couldn't stand this repeated tag line and invariably turned the volume right down until they had finished emoting and up again when they got on with the music. Mike rolled over and blinked.

'Hi Noley. I feel really tired this morning. I don't think I'll get up for a bit.'

'That's fine,' said Noël. 'Take your time. There are no commitments today until teatime when Hilary's coming to measure up for a porch.'

'Hilary?'

'The girl with the lovely smile. Dark bouncy hair.'

'Oh yes. Nice girl.' Mike rolled over and closed his eyes. He hummed a quiet tune under his breath. Noël left him and closed the door quietly. He could get on with things more easily if Mike was not around. Then he felt guilty. Mike might be ill, though he didn't look it – just a bit tired. He'd keep an eye on him. At lunchtime Mike appeared, but still looked sleepy. He dozed on the sofa for most of the afternoon.

Dark clouds rolled across the sky and by teatime the rain had started, gently at first and then a torrent. Noël didn't hear Hilary's car pull up, or her knock at the door. He was in the kitchen buttering some scones that Beth had made that morning when Hilary suddenly appeared in the kitchen doorway.

'Sorry, but I'm afraid I barged in,' she said, taking off her cap and shaking it. 'Good thing you don't lock your front door or I'd have drowned. I can see why you need a porch.'

Noël swung round beaming. He went forward and gave her a hug, then stepped back looking at his shirt-sleeves which were soaked.

'Take your coat off and I'll put it over here to dry,' he said, and busied himself pulling out a chair and hanging her coat over the back so that it could drip on the back-door mat. He could feel warmth in his cheeks, but didn't want her to notice. 'I'll get the kettle on.'

'I've got most of the measurements I need from the original drawings,' said Hilary. 'I just need to know what you want to use the porch for, apart from keeping storms out. Then we can work out the final details.'

Noël felt disappointed. This meant a short visit, he supposed. He took his time finding mugs and plates, then started searching the cupboard for biscuits.

'Let's go through to the hall and I'll bring this lot through,' he said, picking up the tray.

'Mike was dozing when I arrived. I don't think I woke him.'

'Yes, he's very sleepy today. I hope he's OK. He doesn't seem unwell, and ate his lunch as usual.'

Mike woke as they came in. 'Teatime already?' he said, surprised. 'Good.'

'You've been asleep for ages,' said Noël. 'How do you feel now?'

'Absolutely fine,' said Mike, rubbing his eyes. 'Is that strawberry jam on those scones?'

'Yes, made with our own strawberries. Some of them are still fruiting – everything's very odd in the garden this year.'

'I've had another idea for the porch,' said Hilary, 'but it would be quite a lot more expensive. How about making it higher and wider - big enough to include those side windows? Then it would be a sort of sun-room.'

149

'Wouldn't that make the hall dark?' asked Noël.

'Not if we used a lot of glass,' said Hilary. 'Shall I work on that as an alternative idea? Then you can decide which you want to do.'

'It would be good to sit out there in the sunlight,' said Mike. 'I'd like that. Sunlight always makes me feel better. I could put some... some... um... money from what Edgar sends me.'

'I'll get some drawings done then. It shouldn't take long. I'll give you a ring when they're ready.' Too soon Hilary made as if to get up and leave. Noël racked his brains for a delaying tactic but nothing was forthcoming. He went to fetch her damp coat from the kitchen.

'I don't think I'll put that on,' said Hilary. 'I'll just run.' She put on her cap, waved a hand to Mike and Noël and scooted out of the front door.

*

From that day onwards Mike spent most of his mornings in bed. He got up for lunch, but afterwards was still tired and dozed on and off until tea-time. Nothing specific seemed to be wrong with him and the doctor said he had the blood-pressure of a twenty-year old. When there were visitors, or Gerald came to take him out, he managed to do the usual things, but he was much more exhausted afterwards. The only thing that didn't seem to tire him was Emma's lessons. He revelled in explaining the exciting musical ideas that had appeared during the twentieth century. He asked Noël to sort his CDs chronologically, which took a long time and caused several arguments. Beth had given up on helping him.

'I've absolutely no idea whether Stockhausen should come before or after Webern,' she said. 'Not my scene!'

It was left to Noël, who in the end suggested sorting them into blocks of twenty years, by birth date. That didn't make sense musically of course, so in the end they went back to alphabetical order by composer, which was how they were in the first place. Eddie fixed the shelf firmly to the wall, and then kept out of the way.

*

'Frack Off Noël!' shouted Blodwen, pointing towards the Chief's office.

'Hey, what have I done Blod?'

'That's what they're all talking about in there.' Blodwen jerked her thumb towards the editor's office. 'Bloody government's diggin' and frackin' for gas and oil. Seem to have missed the point that we can't go on burnin' stuff. There's something called 'Frack Off' which they're watchin' on the Chief's computer. I think we're doin' a big feature on it. You'd better get in there.'

Noël pushed open the door to the editor's office and found everyone sitting back in their chairs with mugs of coffee.

'Coffee Noël?' said Jean, getting to her feet. 'You've missed the film I'm afraid, but there's a DVD for you to take home.'

'Thanks,' said Noël. 'Any other things for me?'

'A couple of books. One on biochar, and one on living in the woods and building your own house. Really beautiful book that.'

Noël put the books and DVD into his bag. 'I can't stay today I'm afraid. Got the architect coming.'

'Throwing out a wing are you?' asked Peter.

'No, just a porch, or maybe a sun-room. Depends on the design and the cost.'

'Nice,' said Peter.

'How are the First Eleven getting on at your house?'

'You know when Felicity and I moved in there we thought it needed a lot doing to it, but we never got round to it, and we always felt dissatisfied with the place. Now that it's so clean and the garden is being tended I realise that it doesn't need much done to it at all. It's perfect. Emma and company have worked wonders.'

'Do you ever see them when they come round?'

Peter looked slightly embarrassed. 'Yes. I've changed my working days so that I'm there on Wednesdays. It makes it easier. I can make the breakfast and then share it with them. Josie's been showing me the business plan that they are working on with their financial adviser. I was able to suggest a few things he hadn't thought of. She's passed them on. It's looking good and they're hoping that Ivor will join them in the New Year. Then they can widen their offer and diversify their product.'

Noël winced at the unsuitable vocabulary. What the First Eleven did could never be described as a 'product'. It was too alive and intelligent, and unlike anything else. He noted with satisfaction that Peter was smiling much more than he used to. Was there something brewing he wondered. But there was no time to ask as he needed to get home.

'See you next week then Peter.'

Noël had arranged to meet Hilary at The Water Rat, for supper and to see her drawings. Kay and Jim had invited Mike to join them for the evening, and were collecting him by car at five o'clock. Mike got on well with them both, but especially with Kay as her talents and interests were so similar to Mary's. Her embroidery and tapestries were quite different though. Mary's had been cool serene colours and spacious landscapes. Kay used richer tones and her work had more warmth and vibrancy. Noël hurried home to make sure that Mike was awake and ready. He found him dozing on the sofa and woke him gently.

'Time to get ready. You're going to see Kay and Jim this evening.'

It took Mike quite a time to absorb this, but by the time Jim knocked on the door he was more or less ready to go.

'Aren't you coming Noley?'

'Not this time. I've got to meet our architect about the porch, or sun-room. Remember?'

'Tell him to hurry up Noley. It would be good to sit out sometimes.'

'It's not a... Oh yes, I'll say we want to get on with it,' said Noël, not wanting to start on yet another explanation. When Mike had gone he sat down and closed his eyes. Why was it that explanations tired him out so much? It was an hour later when he woke up.

The Water Rat was always cosy in winter. Lights flickered on the rippling river outside the windows, and the little snug at the back had comfortable armchairs and low tables. Hilary was already there when Noël arrived, and she waved to him.

'I got you a pint of Black Sheep,' she said. 'I hope that's right.'

'Just the thing,' said Noël. 'Shall we look at the menu and order supper. Then look at the drawings while we wait?'

'I left the drawings at home,' said Hilary. 'It's so dark here, and there's not much room to spread them out. I thought you might like to see my place anyway after supper. It's so close.'

'Good idea,' said Noël. He had felt resentful when, about ten years ago, some of the old wharf buildings by the canal had been cleared away for the new development. The row of houses and flats had blended in surprisingly well however, and he was curious to see what they were like inside.

After they had eaten they crossed over the road and went through a gateway to the yard by the canal basin. On one side was the large shop where Kay bought her embroidery and tapestry materials. On the other was a small bakery and farm shop where Noël had often bought a sandwich to eat while walking along the towpath. Hilary's house had a garage space on the ground floor with steps up into the living quarters. She led the way up, opened the door and switched on the lights. The main room was white and spacious, with deep blue curtains. There were several bookshelves, a large sofa, an armchair with a soft rug thrown over it, and a round table with four chairs. The drawings were on the table.

'We've more or less definitely decided to make it a sunroom,' said Noël, bending over the drawings. 'Oh yes, that looks great. It fits in perfectly with the gable above and the windows. Brilliant. How soon do you think we could get it done?'

'There's a chap I know who specialises in this sort of thing,' said Hilary. 'I'll give him a ring tomorrow.'

'It will do Mike so much good to be able to sit out there and look at the garden,' said Noël.

'It will be good for you too,' said Hilary quietly.

They sat companionably on the sofa and the talk flowed even more easily than ever before. Hilary was planning a trip to Morocco and showed Noël her maps and guide books.

'Are you going on a guided tour?' asked Noël.

'Oh no! I can't stand being shepherded around in a crowd,' said Hilary. 'I'll just get a return flight to Marrakesh and make it up as I go along. That's how I like to explore a new country.'

'Will you be safe?' asked Noël anxiously.

'Always have been so far,' said Hilary. 'I usually book a place to stay for the first few nights, so that I can get my bearings. Then I like to travel on public transport. You get the feel of the country so much better than being on a coach tour. Most people think I'm a bloke anyway. I usually dress just like this.' Hilary was in her usual jeans and jersey. Her peaked cap was perched on the head of an otter, carved in wood, which sat on one of the bookshelves.

'I've always wanted to go to Morocco,' said Noël. 'It is so near Europe and yet so tremendously different.'

'They speak French of course,' said Hilary. 'That will make it easy to get around. I want to go up into the Atlas mountains, and to see the Sahara.' She paused, biting her lip. Then she turned to face him. 'Why don't you come too?'

'Oh I couldn't leave Mike,' said Noël. 'It wouldn't be fair.'

'Isn't it time you did something just for yourself? I know Mike would understand. He quite likes that Quaker place in Whitby doesn't he?'

'That's true. But... he's getting so frail now. He likes having me around. I don't even like taking these 'respite' weeks really, but I seem to need them. Going off abroad seems irresponsible though.'

Hilary looked down. She didn't want to push the idea too much, and she wasn't quite sure whether it was the right thing to do anyway. Solitary travel suited her, but she knew how much Noël missed his freedom. Maybe she'd mention it again nearer the time. She didn't plan to go until April.

*

'The man from the Council has just been,' said Eddie when Noël got home from town the next day. Noël had been reading and reviewing the Ben Law book on living in the woods, and wished in some ways that this big Victorian pile was a small timber shack among the trees.

'He's happy about the burial site,' continued Eddie. 'There are no watercourse or drainage problems. You just have to register the burial with the Council when the time comes.' For a moment Noël couldn't think what he was talking about. Margot was holding Eddie's hand.

'Daddy was just telling me about dying,' she said. 'Do you know about it Noël?'

'I've got a rough idea,' said Noël, wondering how Eddie had handled the subject.

'Well,' said Margot, standing facing Noël confidently. 'You die when you've had *all* your happy. Isn't that right Daddy?'

'It's about right,' said Eddie smiling down at her and running his fingers through her hair. Margot ran off happily, her red boots splashing in the puddles on the drive.

154

'She was here when the Council officer came,' said Eddie. 'We hadn't talked about death much before, but she had been asking questions about a dead starling that we found yesterday, so today was quite a good time to tell her a bit more. She was interested, but not upset.'

'Children are amazing,' said Noël. 'So straightforward.'

38. Spring again

It was the first really warm day that year. The daffodils were just beginning to show a hint of yellow. The rain that had fallen the night before was sparkling along the twigs of the cherry tree. Noël sat on the new wooden seat which they had put at the edge of the hill. The river curved away below just as it always had. Beside him a single snowdrop shone in the middle of a neatly raked patch of earth. He felt as if something inside him had dropped away, like the houses that fell into the sea at Whitby last year. His mind was completely blank and hollowed out. It had all been so sudden. Only two weeks ago the sun-room had been finished. The slender white supports held the canopy of glass in graceful panels. They had found a couple of comfortable loungers and Mike had sat there on that first morning with his feet up, a rug over his lap.

'Hey Noley this is great! The hall is great too, but the sunlight here is something else.' He lay back and closed his eyes. 'Tell Margot I'll read her a story out here after lunch.'

Noël had made a thick broccoli and Stilton soup with chunks of soft wholemeal bread, and they had eaten on their laps in the sunshine. Margot had skipped in with her favourite book, the one with the two rabbits on the cover. Noël took the dishes in to the kitchen to wash up and Margot curled up on Noël's chair. Knowing Mike was happily occupied Noël set about preparing the vegetables for supper. Then he decided to make a pancake mixture for one of Mike's favourite puddings. He took a quick look out through the front door and Margot was curled up asleep in his chair. Mike was sleeping too with the book in his hand. Noël smiled and went back to whizz up the flour, eggs and milk and set it aside to blend. He put out a couple of lemons and some maple syrup. Sitting down at the kitchen table he picked up the newspaper. After a while he heard a slight sound and Margot came tiptoeing into the room.

'Noël,' she said softly. 'Come and see Mike. I think he's had all his happy.'

Noël smiled absently, put the paper down and took her hand. 'OK, let's go and see him.' They went across the hall and out of the front door. Mike was still lying back with his eyes partly closed. The book he had been reading to Margot had slipped out of his hand on to the floor. Noël stiffened. He put his hand out to touch Mike's, and knew straight away.

Margot smiled and bent to pick up her book. It was called 'Guess How Much I Love You.'

'He finished the story though,' she said. 'That's good.'

*

Hilary looked across the garden at the slumped figure silhouetted against the sky. She felt the sharp edges of the travel documents in her pocket. Was it too soon to talk about Morocco? As she watched, Noël straightened up and appeared to be listening intently. A curlew curved across the sky and its wild solitary call sliced through the air. She moved softly across the grass and slid on to the seat beside him. He turned and his eyes had regained some of their shine.

'Did you hear that?'

Hilary nodded.

'Every spring when I hear the curlew it lifts my heart.'

'New beginnings,' she said quietly. 'Can I give you these?' She slipped a paper folder into his hands.

'Tickets for Morocco – going overland through Spain. I'm afraid I took an executive decision. I hope you don't mind.'

Noël looked blankly at the red and green folder, then shook his head. Hilary held her breath.

'I can't believe it,' he sighed at last. 'I just can't believe how good life can be.'

'Is it OK then?' she asked. 'Will you come? Shall we go exploring?'

They both stood up and Noël felt blindly for Hilary's hand. They walked silently across the grass together towards the house.

Books, DVDs and Music mentioned in the text

BOOKS
**Most of these books and DVDs are available from
www.green-shopping.co.uk**
Boyle, Mark – The Moneyless Manifesto (2012)
Daly, Herman – Steady State Economics: The Economics of
Biophysical Equilibrium and Moral Growth (1977)
 – Beyond Growth: Economics of Sustainable Development
(1997)
Eisenstein, Charles – The Rise of Humanity: Civilization (sic)
and the Human Sense of Self (2007, 2013)
Fermor, Patrick Leigh – A Time of Gifts (1977)
Hawken, Paul – Blessed Unrest: How the Largest Movement
in the World came into Being and why No One saw it Coming.
(2008)
Hodgkinson, Tom – How to be Free (2006)
Lasn, Kalle ed. - Meme Wars: The Creative Destruction of
Neo-classical Economics (2012)
Lewis, Martin – Thrifty Ways for Modern Days (2006)
McBratney & Jeram – Guess How Much I Love You
Macy, Joanna and Johnstone, Chris – Active Hope: How to
face the Mess We're in Without Going Crazy (2012)
Meadows, Donella et al – The Limits to Growth (1972)
Mortimer, John – Summer of a Dormouse: A Year of Growing
Old Disgracefully (2000)
Pollan, Michael – Food Rules: an Eater's Manual (2010)
Schumacher, E.F. – Small is Beautiful: A Study of Economics
as if People Mattered (1974)

DVDs
Ancient Futures: Learning from Ladakh
 together with Paradise with Side Effects(1993)
Food Inc (2009)
Positive Money – Ben Dyson

MUSIC
Beethoven – Symphony No.4 in Bb Op.60
Beethoven – Equali for four trombones WoO30
Borodin – Overture 'Prince Igor'
Brahms – String Quartet in c minor Op.51 No.1
Butterworth – 'The Banks of Green Willow'
Dvořák – Symphony No.9 'From the New World'
Ives – The Unanswered Question
Mendelssohn – Octet
Ravel – 'Daphnis et Chloë'
Ravel – Le Tombeau de Couperin
Sibelius – The Swan of Tuonela
Sibelius – En Saga
Stravinsky – The Rite of Spring
Tchaikovsky – Overture 1812
Tchaikovsky – Symphony No.4
Tchaikovsky – Symphony No. 6 'Pathétique'
Tomasi – Le Petit Chevrier Corse
Vivaldi – The Four Seasons
Wagner – The Ride of the Valkyries from 'Die Walküre'

Acknowledgements

This story arrived of its own accord. Each week another incident or character would appear and I was constantly being surprised, or horrified, by them. At the end of the year it finished itself quietly and I put it on one side. My friend Christine Muskett asked to read it, and having enjoyed it, and spotted all the missing commas, asked if she could pass it on to someone who didn't know me. She chose James Partridge, CEO of the charity 'Changing Faces'. It was his reaction that convinced me that it was in fact a book, and publishable. Most of all I would like to thank all the extraordinary and wonderful people I've met during my life, not least my dear partner David Morris. None of them are depicted in the story, but many of their characteristics have been shared around by the characters in unexpected ways.
June Emerson, North Yorkshire 2014

31857091R00094

Made in the USA
Charleston, SC
31 July 2014